Denmark! Where's That Then?

A J Bowes

For Maisie

Preface

I wrote this book for you, lads.
Yes, sorry ladies, but there are endless books out there for
you. Romance, dramas, thrillers with intricately-woven
plots, non-fiction tales of women who conquered
adversary – the list is endless!
When we go on holiday and we're sat by the pool, you girls
have a lovely little stack of books to get through, and don't
appreciate it very much when we start pestering you to
entertain us. So I thought us guys needed a little book to
keep us all out of mischief while we sit next to our better
half's and replenish their drinks.
Don't get me wrong, ladies may absolutely love this book,
but I didn't write it for you, so hands off!

Breakfast at Maisie's

I lay in bed with my eyes closed, wondering what time it was.

I was trying to stretch my legs but the bed was too short, so I swung them out of the side.

Bloody 'ell, it's cold!

I quickly drew my legs back under the blankets and curled them up again.

Outside the door, I heard the floorboards creak and my Mam whispered to the dog, "C'mon Butch, let's get you outside for a wee."

I knew then that it must only be about five or six o'clock, because Mam got up at roughly the same time every morning.

I followed her descent down the stairs in my mind, listening to the tell-tale creak of the odd offending step until she reached the bottom. She turned the key in the lock and opened the front door.

"Go on, go for a wee," she encouraged. I felt sorry for him, going out into the dark, cold, November morning. "And don't be scratching at the door or bloody barkin' to come in after!" she whispered to him, as if he could understand.

Maybe he could?

I squinted at my watch through the darkness, and the illuminous dial told me that it was five forty.

Oh, good. I've got nearly an hour an' half before I have to get up.

I reset my head into the pillow and tried to get back to sleep.

Suddenly, the bed creaked and moved.

I opened my eyes with a start and looked up at the underside of the top bunk that my younger brother was sleeping in.

We shoulda got new beds ages ago.

Lew and I had slept in these beds since I was in junior school and now we were both working. When I'm out and about it's not on my mind, but then I get back in bed and I have the same thoughts over and over again.

One day, they'll just collapse and then we'll wish we'd have done somethin' about it.

I closed my eyes, thinking about last night when we were out drinking with Pop.

The bed creaked again.

I opened one eye and waited.

Is this it? Is this the mornin' they collapse?

There was a brief silence, and then Lewis let out an extraordinarily loud, long fart, followed by a muffled cough and a grunt.

Smelly get.

I turned my head back to the wall, snuggled into my pillow, and gently drifted back to sleep.

"Jack... Lewis! Come on, get up, it's seven o 'clock," my Mam called ever so quietly, as if she was afraid that we were actually going to wake up. I was awake already, but it was so warm and comfortable in my bed that I was reluctant to leave it.

"Are you up?" she whispered near my head. Mam still treated me like I was two years old, but I wouldn't change her for the world. "Bloody 'ell, it stinks in here!" I opened my eyes slightly to see her face screwed up. I stifled a laugh.

You'd think she'd be used to it by now, with five lads to look after! Well, six if you include Pop.

"It's him," mumbled Lewis sleepily, "fartin' all night!"

"Well, I'm openin' the window, let some fresh air in," replied Maisie.

"Oh! Don't Mam, its bloody freezin' in here as it is!" I moaned, raising my head off the pillow and out to glare at Lewis on the top bunk. "And don't you blame it all on me!"

"It's the both o' you," Mam chastised gently, "what were you drinkin' last night anyway?"

Lew looked at me for help. "Dunno," he said "but we met Pop in the Red Rose, he was buyin' the drinks."

"Oh aye, he's had a lickle win on the pools," said Maisie. Lewis grinned, pleased with himself for shifting the blame over to Pop for buying the drinks, and therefore he wasn't at fault for the odour in the bedroom. "He said he's gonna take me to the Con Club on Saturday."

"Con Club?" I was surprised, because Pop hated conservatives, especially Margaret Thatcher. "What's he takin' you there for?"

"Well, I know he's not best fond of 'em, but it's a lovely club really, much better than the Labour one. Now come on, get up! Your brew's goin' cold!" Her tone implied that small talk was over.

Ah, good-old Maisie.

She left our room and I dragged myself out of bed with my head ducked, but I still hit the bottom rail of Lewis' bed. "You do that every mornin', nobhead." I stomped over to the window and slammed it shut. Lewis jumped off his bunk and headed out of the door. "It's still bloody freezin' in here," he moaned, walking down the hall to the bathroom. I turned and got a glimpse of his hairy arse peeking out of a hole in his frayed, off-white boxers.

3

"Maybe you should buy some new undies then, if you're cold. Scruffy get."

The bathroom in our house was the only room with a lock, so it was a good place to seek refuge from an angry brother. No matter how old we were, it was surprising how often it was used as a safe haven. Even to this day, I'm sure Pop uses it as his sanctuary too. The door bore undulations in the flat veneer where Pop had papered and painted over the holes and dents caused by our fighting. He used to remark that the toilet door had seen more action than some soldiers.

I walked into the spacious living room to the wonderful smell of toast coming from the kitchen, where Maisie was making breakfast. The rectangular-shaped room had a fireplace embedded on the left wall with two wide windows facing opposite each other overlooking the front and back gardens. A wide settee sat opposite the fireplace and one of the single-seaters was positioned underneath the front window. The other single-seater, which had always been Pop's chair, lived next to Maisie's spot on the corner of the settee, adjacent to the kitchen door. At the back of the house, the dining table was set under the window behind Pop's chair.

Home.

Two cups of tea waited for us on the table. I looked out of the window to the back garden and saw Butch sitting on the grass. He was staring intently toward the garden fence, as though expecting someone.

I sat down and watched Mam make our breakfast in the kitchen through the open door. She was a beautiful woman with short, curly hair and a pretty face. Not a wrinkle in sight. As with most women, she felt like she was a little overweight, courtesy of bearing five sons, she'd say.

'One day I'll be slim again, like I was when I met your Dad.'

I could hear the tell-tale heavy scraping of a knife on

toast. "You burnt 'em again, Mam?"

"Well, just a lickle bit 'round the edges, you want me put some more in?"

"Yeah please, give *them* to Lewis," I chuckled, sipping my tea.

Mam had retired last year because my brothers and I had said that, since we were all working, she should finish work and take it easy. Of course, in true Maisie fashion, she never did. She was always doing something. She used to love going to work, being with the girls, and having a good gossip. Maisie suffered from Byssinosis, a type of lung disease, due to working in the cotton mills all her life. She also had Type 1 diabetes and only one kidney, but she was tough as old boots, our Mam.

We made sure that she had enough money for herself and the housekeeping, because she wasn't yet old enough for her state pension. Neither was Pop, but he managed well with his job, four days a week. He worked as branch secretary of the GMBU (General, Municipal Boiler Maker's Union) North West, which paid a decent wage and he thoroughly enjoyed it.

"Who was in the toilet last?" asked Pop, walking into the living room clutching the day's newspaper. "It bloody stinks!"

"Lew," I said, taking a bite of my toast, staring down at the table.

"It's not just Lewis, it's the pair of you," said Maisie curtly, "they're both bloody rotten this mornin', Frank. What were you makin' them drink last night?"

Pop looked over at me with his eyebrows furrowed, put his finger to his lips and shook his head. "Er – they were just on shandy, love."

Maisie shook her head and smiled. "Do you want some toast and a brew, Frank?"

"No toast, thanks love, just a brew. I'm gonna get the ten to eight bus, go in a bit earlier."

Pop was a tall, lean man with short, greying hair. He

moved with a military bearing, courtesy of the British Army, where he served his time as a tank commander in the Suez crisis. During the conflict, his regiment suffered an attack from a lone sniper whilst on a rest period in what was supposed to be a safe zone. Pop was the only person who got shot – in his leg. The other soldiers acted swiftly and apprehended the sniper, who turned out to be a nine year old boy. He always joked that had the boy been a little taller, we might never have been born.

Since Pop's leg suffered a serious wound, the British medical field staff told him that they would have to amputate. Luckily, there was an American surgeon on secondment to the British army in attendance as they did the rounds, and he said that it wasn't necessary to amputate – he could operate and save the leg. As they say, the rest is history, and he still has two perfectly good legs to this day.

My older brother was Stuart and he worked in engineering. He recently got married to his childhood sweetheart and moved out. We didn't see much of him after that. The rest of us still lived at home, which made me the oldest lad in the house. Eric and Cliff followed Mam into the cotton industry, and Lewis decided to come and work with me at the farm.

Lewis walked into the living room and called out, "Where's me brew Mam?"

"On the table," she said, "with your toast."

"Bloody 'ell, Mam!" cried Lewis. "Why don't you get a job at the Crematorium?"

"Hey! Cheeky bugger," she said under her breath, as she continued pottering about in the kitchen. Lewis leaned in towards me.

"It's burnt to death, this toast," he whined.

"Oh, just get 'em eaten."

"I bet your toast weren't burnt, eh?" A snide look crossed his face. "Ooh! Can't give best baby burnt toast, can we?" he mocked.

6

"Piss off."

"Hey! Pack it in and get to work you two!" Mam shouted. Lewis and I glared at each other.

Lewis always knew how to wind me up. Whether intentionally or not, he just knew how to do it. It must be an age thing, because the oldest and the youngest of any family are always a pain in the arse. Thank God I was neither.

We tended to get on quite well and I thought it was because we were very similar, but that could also be the reason we bickered so often. He may not have been the strongest looking lad on the estate, but he was certainly the cockiest.

And he was *my* little brother.

"Right, I'm off love," Pop said, giving Maisie a kiss. "You two get to work, you don't wanna be late and upset Dougal Arse, do you?" he said, smiling as he walked through the door.

"I think I'll put some washin' on." Mam was off talking to herself again, but she raised her voice and asked, "Have you two got any washin' upstairs?"

"No," we both said in unison. If we said yes, we know she'd ask us to go upstairs and get it, and I for one couldn't be bothered with that. Neither could Lew. We both made our way towards the back door, past Mam in the kitchen. She turned.

"Are you sure?"

"Yeah Mam, see you later."

"Ta-ra." We mumbled, leaving the house.

Just before I closed the door I heard her say, "Lyin' buggers."

Dougal Arse

The sky was just beginning to brighten as we climbed into my beloved, yellow Fiat 132 saloon. There was rust all over the bodywork, reminding me that she'd seen better days, but I just couldn't bear to get rid of her. I loved that car. She was mechanically sound, but the body was rotten. I knew that the day would come when I'd have to part with her, but I tended not to think about it, if I could help it.

I turned the key and the engine fired into life with a slight roaring sound.

Just like a Ferrari.

I smiled. It took less than five minutes to get to the farm from home, and we could've walked.

But why walk when you have a car, eh!

Meadow Heights Farm was owned by the Mellor family.

Mrs Katherine Mellor had brought up two young children by herself and managed to sell produce out of one of the stables, turning a run-down farm into a thriving business. She was a very strong-willed woman, who didn't think twice about speaking her mind.

Katherine's children, Douglas and Sally, now ran the business. Since they had taken over, the company had branched out to include plant hire and construction, as well as the farm shop.

When we got to the farm, we headed straight for the Portakabin, which doubled as an office and a canteen.

Paul was already there. He'd worked at the farm driving the hire plant machinery for about four years. He was sat at the table, drinking tea from a thermos. His round belly, which was bulging out of his open overalls, was rubbing against the table.

"Alright Paul?" I asked, smiling at him.

"Aye," he said, taking a sip of tea.

"Dougal Arse up yet?" Lew asked, pulling on his own overalls.

"Is he bollocks," Paul wiped a dribble of tea from his beard as he spoke, "you know what he's like."

"What you on today, Paul?"

"JCB for Gavin Hulme, diggin' foundations for an extension."

"At least you'll have an easy day, then?"

"Hopefully."

"I'm on for Paul England, cartin' soil to the tip."

"Oh aye!" I said, "How much you rippin' Paul England off for then?"

Lewis drove a tractor and trailer at the farm, so most of the time he was hired out to various builders and landscapers to transport unwanted soil off their sites to a landfill area. The chap in charge of the landfill was named Eric. He was a miserable bloke in his late fifties, very scruffy-looking, with the most unfortunate complexion. Hence Lewis's nickname for him - Boilly Eric.

One of Lewis's earlier visits to Boilly Eric's tip had seen them come to an agreement that Lewis would pay Eric in cash, since the farm didn't have an account with the tip owners. The tip fee would be twenty pounds per load, but Lewis would tell the people he was on hire to that it was twenty-five pounds, so that he had a nice little profit of five pounds per load.

Lewis loved it when he was out on this sort of work. The only person who didn't know about his little business venture was Douglas. He would have hit the roof had he known, because he would want the money, even though he was getting paid separately for the hire of Lewis, the tractor, and the trailer. But money was Douglas's God, as his mother repeatedly told him.

"What you on about?" said Lewis.

"Whatever," I said, smiling over at Paul.

"What you doin' today, Bert?" Paul asked me.

"I've got a job to price for Tameside Council."

"What is it?"

"Oh, the usual," I said, "flaggin' and that."

"Better than nowt, innit?"

Bert was short for Albert.

It was a name I had picked up on a night out with the lads in Manchester City Centre. We had been chatting to a group of Irish girls who were over for a hen party. One girl in particular had caught my eye and I spent quite a bit of time trying to talk to her. It was really loud in the pub, and with the lads interrupting us every chance they got, we found it a bit difficult to hear each other.

The lads and I eventually decided to leave the girls to it. We said our goodbyes and headed out of the pub. I turned to wave as I got to the door and the girl I had been chatting to shouted, "Bye Albert, it was lovely to meet you!"

All the Irish girls shouted in unison, "Ooh! Bye Albert!" And they fell over each other giggling.

"What did she just call me then?" I asked as we walked away.

"Albert," Lewis replied.

"Fuckin' Albert? Where the bloody 'ell did she get Albert from? Did one of you buggers tell her I was called Albert?"

"Dunno, but it suits you, Alberts are always miserable buggers!"

So the name stuck.

"Mornin'," Douglas said, in his usual world-on-his-shoulders voice, sauntering into the office.

"Mornin'," we all chorused.

"What you still doin' here, Lewis?"

"I'm just goin'-" Lewis said, looking at Douglas.

"Well, go on then," Douglas said sternly.

"Wanker," whispered Lew under his breath, turning to leave.

Paul got up without saying a word and made his way over to the JCB. Once alone, Douglas turned to me. "What you up to today?" he asked.

"Pricin' that Tameside job."

"Leave that, I need you to help me with the Christmas tree order."

I knew what that meant. Douglas didn't do anything himself, just in case it turned out to be wrong. So if there was a problem, he always had someone to blame other than himself. "I thought you'd already done it?" I asked, knowing full well he hadn't. He was on the defensive immediately.

"I've been busy," he muttered.

Busy, my arse.

"Johansens wanted the amounts last week, so they could get our order sorted," I said, provoking Douglas more as I tried to make a point of what a useless bugger he was.

"So why haven't you done them?" Douglas asked.

"Why haven't *I* done- ?" I knew it was a waste of time arguing, so I just sat back down and went through the order with Douglas.

Armed with the order information, he headed out to phone Dan at Johansens and place the order from the phone inside the farmhouse. He never used the phone in the office when he was buying anything, because he didn't want anyone to know how much he was actually paying.

Johansens were a company based in Padborg in Denmark, on the border with Germany. We had been dealing with them for a number of years, buying Nordmann fir Christmas trees. A few years ago, the Nordmann fir grew in popularity, and were now the new, must-have tree, because of their needle-retaining capabilities and conventional shape. They were only grown prolifically in Denmark, so the Danes had quite a monopoly on sales and price. Johansens would ship an unaccompanied trailer load over to Newcastle, where it was met by a British haulier and delivered to Meadow Heights.

Easy.

I pulled the file marked TMBC out of the filing cabinet, sat down at my desk and started to peruse the bill of quantities.

'Item 1.1: Remove all existing Stone setts to the rear of Green Lane, house numbers 23-56 and dispose of at contractors tip. Item 1.2: Excavate to reduce levels and remove arisings to–'

I was interrupted as I heard Douglas shouting from the yard.

"Jack! JACK!" There was an anxious note in his voice. I got up and went outside to see what was going on, nearly running into Douglas as he came crashing through the door.

"You'll never guess what's happened now!"

"What?"

"I knew this'd happen," he said, "fuckin' knew it! *You* should've sorted this out last week."

"What the fuck are you talkin' about?" I was angry now.

"We can't have any trees."

"What d'you mean?"

Douglas explained that when he phoned Dan at Johansens to place the order, he said that it was too late to arrange transport to the UK, so he couldn't supply the trees. "Y'know what I think?" Douglas said, "y'know that bloody Berlin wall came down last year, didn't it?"

Where's he going with this?

"And?"

"And," said Douglas nastily, "I reckon they're sendin' *my* trees to East Germany instead of sendin' them here."

"Well, why would they do that?" I couldn't understand his logic.

"Because they'll get more money for 'em, won't they?"

My eyebrows shot up. "You really think that's the case?"

"I'm bloody certain."

"So, what do we do now?" I asked him, scratching my head.

"Dunno. I knew this'd happen." Douglas always knew when something was going to happen after it had already happened, he was just that type. "I'm gonna lose loads of money this year without them trees! That's all they want now, them Nordmann, and if I go the wholesale market to buy them, there'll be no profit for me."

What a shame.

"So – hold on – Dan didn't say that they had no trees, just that he couldn't organise transport?"

"Yeah, so what?"

"So, ring him back and see if we can go and get 'em."

"Don't be so bloody stupid," Douglas spat.

"Why? If we're picking them up, surely you can negotiate a better price, and you'll get more out've them." Not that I cared too much about making him any more money, but it was the only idea that got us what we wanted with minimal fuss. I could almost see the pound signs in Douglas's eyes as he thought it through.

"Right, I'll ring him back." He said with a new

determination.

And off he skipped.

I returned to my desk and started to read the bill of quantities again.

Right. 'Item 1.1: Remove all existing Stone setts to the rear of Green Lane-'

Oh! It's no good, I can't concentrate! What if Dan says yeah, come and collect the trees? What the hell am I gonna go in?

Can't go in Big Edith! That old bastard'll never get there. We'll have to hire a tractor unit, a new Volvo or Scania. Ooh, now that'd be nice – oh, shut up, it won't happen anyway!

'Item 1.1: Remove all existing Stone setts from-' Bugger it!

I need to have a look at this job before I can put any prices to it. Might as well go now.

I stood up, gathered all the paperwork together and started to move towards the office door when Douglas came bounding in again.

"Where you goin'?" he said, with a broad grin on his face.

"Green Lane, to look at this job," I replied, holding the documents up.

"Oh no you're not, you're off to Denmark."

"What?"

"You're on! I've just negotiated the best price ever!" He was hardly able to contain himself. "Half price – half fuckin' price!"

"So, what now?"

"Well, you better start organisin' yourself to go."

"First of all we'll need to hire a tractor unit and a trailer," I told him, wiping the smile off his face. "I'll ring up Salford Van Hire an' get a price."

"Woah! We've got a tractor unit and a trailer!"

The tractor unit owned by Meadow Heights farm was an eleven-year-old ERF, nicknamed Big Edith. I usually drove it around the UK, picking up potatoes and vegetables for the farm shop and some wholesale market customers. It was also used, when coupled to a low-loader trailer, for delivering dumpers and small plant to builders.

"What? Big Edith? That fuckin' thing won't get to Denmark!"

"Course it will, just give it a service today."

"Service! But I thought we might hire a new Volvo, or Scania, or summat…" I could see it was useless before I began, but I still asked anyway.

"Fuck that," said Douglas, "cost too much. Anyway, that's Swedish rubbish. ERF – good old British engineerin'. Get you to China and back that truck will."

"Well, I'm gonna need a hand gettin' things organised."

"I'm too busy," he said immediately. I rolled my eyes. Just at that moment however, Paul wandered back into the office. "What you doin' back?"

"Job's been called off," Paul told us, "buildin' inspector can't come out 'til tomorrow, so they won't let me dig the foundations 'cause they don't wanna leave 'em overnight."

"Right, Paul you go and take over from Lewis, and tell him to come back here an' help Jack." Paul didn't question it, he just set off in the direction of the work's van, while I walked into the barn to look at Big Edith.

"Well girl, I've gone and done it now." I started to jack up the cab when Douglas appeared at the side of me.

"Right, I'm off out," he said, pulling on his coat. "Oh! Has your Lew got a passport?"

"Yeah."

"Good, 'cause he can go with you," he muttered as he climbed into his Mercedes.

Why Me?

I was well underway servicing Big Edith when Lewis came into the barn.

"Why didya send Paul up to take over from me?" he demanded. "I've only done two loads this mornin'."

"You mean you've only earned ten quid this mornin'," I clarified.

"What d'you mean?" he asked innocently.

"Everyone knows about your scams, apart from Dougal Arse," I laughed.

"Well, thanks to you, Paul definitely knows now, I had to tell the fat sod."

"Oh aye, he'll be reet in the pie shop at lunchtime with your money!"

"Get stuffed. What've you got me back for anyway? I hope it's not to help you service this old bastard," he gestured at Big Edith.

"Well, actually it is," I grinned, playing with him because I knew he was really pissed off with having to give his scam away to Paul.

I put my head back down underneath the big cab and set about loosening the alternator so I could fit new drive belts. I was leaving nothing to chance with Big Edith. She was having a service like never before.

I bet she thinks it's her birthday!

Engine oil change, new filters, alternator drive belts, hoses to the cooling system. The works!

"You got me back here to fuck about with this?" said Lewis, kicking the front wheel. "You know I'm no good at bein' a mechanic, and I fuckin' hate gettin' full of oil – that shit gets under your nails and everywhere!"

"Aww, an' you've just had your nails done, haven't you?" I teased.

"Well, fuck Dougal Arse!" he exclaimed angrily, turning to walk out of the barn. "I'm goin' back to me job – Paul can help you piss about with Big Edith."

"Lew!" I shouted after him. He didn't look around, he just put two fingers up over his shoulder. "Lewis, remember when I told you to get a passport last year?"

He stopped, turned around and said, "What? Fuckin' passport? What's that gotta do with 'owt?"

"Come back in here and I'll tell you," I said. I watched him drag his feet as he came back, stuffing his hands in his pockets.

"Go on then," he grumbled, still looking disgruntled.

"You and me our kid, are goin' to Denmark."

"Denmark! Where's that then?"

I told him the situation and that we would be leaving the next morning. His mood changed almost immediately.

"Bloody 'ell!"

He was smiling at last.

Once I had finished all the major parts of the service I left Lewis to tidy up, check the tyre pressures, and grease the steering components and suspension.

Meanwhile, I went in search of a TILT type trailer to transport the Christmas trees in. I'd finally managed to persuade Dougal Arse to hire one, explaining that the two trailers we had weren't suitable to transport one thousand, two hundred Christmas trees in, and that it would be more practical to load the trees into a TILT. I had found a company in Trafford Park – thanks to the good old Yellow Pages – called Central Trailers, who agreed to hire us a TILT trailer, assuming that the rushed account application could be authorised in time.

Lewis was giving Big Edith a much needed wash when Dougal Arse drove back into the yard. He got out of his car and motioned for me to follow him into the office. He had a furtive look on his face and I could clearly see something tucked under his jumper.

"Sit down," he closed the office door behind me. I took a seat and looked into Douglas's serious face.

What's all this about?

He peered through the window to reassure himself that nobody was looking in and sat down opposite me. He gave one last look around and produced a blue, cotton, Barclays bag from under his jumper. "That's the money," he said, pushing the bag toward me.

"What money?" I asked, looking down at the bag.

"For the trees!" Douglas hissed, as though I were missing something very obvious.

"What? I've gotta take *cash* all the way to Denmark? Can't you just transfer it to their bank?"

"Well, if the trees are no good when you get there, they'll have my money and I won't have any bargainin' power, will I?"

"Okay then, transfer it when we're loaded and happy with the quality." I countered.

"That won't work," he shook his head, a frown appearing on his brow. "I've asked at the bank and the money could take a week to clear, with it being an international transaction, so you'd be sat in Denmark until the money cleared."

Sounds alright to me.

"Anyway, you'll need cash to pay the VAT at customs when you come back."

We discussed the pros and cons of taking cash, but eventually agreed that it was the only option, given the time schedule. "How much is in the bag?" I asked.

"Ten grand."

"Fuck me!" I looked at the bag again, sitting on the desk.

Lewis and I could just fuck off to Benidorm with that!

Douglas gave me copies of the costings from Dan at Johansens and the VAT costs. "You should have enough with ten grand," he assured me, "with a few hundred to spare." He also gave me six hundred pounds for food, lodging, and emergencies. "Don't tell your Lew that you've got all that money. Thievin' bugger'll nick it," he added.

"Hey!" I said, in Lewis' defence.

"You know what I mean."

I didn't know what he meant actually.

Does he know about Lewis's scams?

"Is it all in there?" I asked, nodding towards the bag.

"To the penny, I've counted it three times."

I believed him. The only part I didn't believe was that he had only counted it three times.

Douglas got up to leave the office. "What about diesel?"

"Oh yeah, forgot about that. Could you use your credit card and I'll give you the money when you get back?"

Fair enough, we'll have enough cash with us – we don't want any more.

"Oh!" I'd just remembered. "The passenger door doesn't lock on Big Edith."

"Well, get a new part," Douglas said.

"I've tried, but they can't get the part in 'til next week."

"Well, you'd better not let that money out of your sight then," he closed the door as he left.

I looked down at the blue Barclays bag full of money.

What the fuck am I gonna put this in?

I didn't like the idea of putting it up my jumper like Douglas, or in the travel bag I would be taking with me.

I scanned the office, hoping to get some inspiration, when my eyes fell upon my old Delsey briefcase.

Perfect.

It was made of black, rigid, plastic with two locking clasps, which I still had the keys for. I pulled it out from between two filing cabinets, noticing that it looked a little worse for wear. It had deep scratch marks here and there, from where it had been thrown in and out of the work's van, and smears of mud, clay, and other unknown substances all over it. I had used the briefcase to carry documents when we did contracting work, as it kept them clean and flat. Now it would be tasked with a much more important job.

I emptied it and cleaned it up as best I could. Oddly enough, I found a packet of Wine Gums inside.

I can't remember putting them in here.

But they tasted alright, so I munched away while I placed the money and documents into the briefcase and locked it up.

I'm surprised Dougal Arse hasn't made me handcuff it to my wrist. Better not mention it, or the bugger'll make me do it.

I started laughing to myself.

I phoned Central Trailers, hoping our application had been successful, because if not it'd be a bit of a disaster. Thankfully everything was fine, and we were clear to collect the trailer in the morning. The ferry was booked – Dover to Ostend in Belgium – and everything was good to go.

"Reet our Bert," called Lewis as he walked into the office, "Big Edith's washed, full of diesel, and ready to go."

"Good lad, we need to get home and sort our stuff out."

"Sounds good to me!" Lewis replied enthusiastically. I knew how he felt, I was excited too. But I couldn't help feeling a little apprehensive. I had a strange feeling that things weren't going to be easy.

We didn't sleep much that night. We lay in our bunk beds talking about where we were going and what might happen. We were like two little kids, excited about going on a school trip in the morning.

Manky Margaret

My alarm went off at seven o'clock, as usual.

"Come on Jack, get up," Maisie whispered in my ear. I didn't need any inspiration to get out of bed this morning.

"C'mon Lew!" I called, crawling out of the bottom bunk.

"He's already downstairs," said Maisie, leaving the bedroom.

Bloody 'ell, he's keen.

When I entered the living room, Lewis was sat at the table with his coat on and his travel bag between his feet.

"You ready Bert?" Lewis asked.

"Bloody 'ell, gimme a chance," I replied, smiling. "Let me have a brew and a smoke first."

When we were ready to go we picked up our bags, including the one Mam had prepared for us with emergency food in.

"If you haven't got it, you can't eat it, can you?" she told us.

We also got a quick lecture about looking after each other before we managed to escape through the back door.

When our bags, including the briefcase, were safely in the boot of the car, we got in and buckled up.

Further down the road, we saw Pop walking back from the shop with his newspaper under his arm and Butch alongside him. I started my Ferrari and drove toward them. Lewis wound the window down and Butch jumped up at the car. Pop ducked his head so he could see though the open window and I looked over at him, expecting another lecture.

"Have a good time, drive carefully, and bring me a bottle of whisky back," he said, smiling. "C'mon Butch," Pop started walking away, "I'm touchin' bloody cloth here!" It wasn't that Pop didn't care, he just didn't make a fuss.

"See you later!" we both shouted, and I sped off down the road.

The gates were already open at the farm.

Paul must have gone out early with the JCB to the job he had to abandon yesterday.

"C'mon," I said to Lewis, "let's get our stuff loaded into Big Edith before Dougal Arse gets up, I can't be bothered with that pillock this mornin'."

As I was stacking the bags on the bunk, I noticed Douglas's bedroom window opening.

Fuck's sake. That's the last thing I need.

"Jack, Jack!" Douglas shouted. I climbed down out of the cab and went around to the side of the truck so I could see him.

"What?" I asked.

"Come over 'ere," he said, beckoning me through the open window in his sleeveless vest.

Aww, no pyjamas, Dougal Arse?

"What?" I asked again.

"Have you still got that money?" he whispered.

No, me and Lewis went on the piss with it last night, what do you think?

"Yeah, course I have, why? Don't you trust me?" I was trying to make him feel bad for asking.

"Yeah, 'course I do," he said sheepishly, "it's just that it's a lot o' money."

"Don't worry, it'll be safe with Lewis," I started walking back to the truck, smiling.

"That's what I'm fuckin' worried about!" he said, agitated. "Ring me when you get chance and let me know how you're gettin' on."

"Ok."

"What's up with her?" asked Lewis, nodding toward Douglas.

"Oh, just the usual," I replied, "c'mon, let's fuck off before he starts mitherin' us again." I started Big Edith's engine, looked over to Lewis and asked, "You ready, our kid?"

He looked at me, smiled and said, "Dunno."

I slipped Big Edith into gear and drove out of the farmyard.

"Is it far?" Lewis asked me.

"Is what far?"

"Trafford Park."

"Nah, about half an hour or so."

It probably would have been half an hour if we were driving in the evening, but as it was eight o'clock in the morning we got tangled up in rush hour traffic. So it was quarter to ten before we arrived at Central Trailers.

We drove in through the big, steel, mesh gates and saw line upon line of TILT trailers parked up ready to go; some new, some not so new, some old, and some really old ones.

"What d'you reckon?" I said to Lewis, nodding toward the lines of trailers.

"What?"

24

"D'you think we'll get a new one? Or one of them old buggers?"

"Knowin' our luck," said Lewis laughing, "probably an old bugger."

I parked up outside the offices and told Lewis to keep an eye on the truck. Once inside I got all the necessary documentation and was about to leave when the guy who had been dealing with me asked where we were going. I told him the story and he raised his eyebrows, wished us the best of luck, and shook my hand. I thanked him and walked out to the truck with the same uneasy feeling I had from the previous night. It seemed he knew something we didn't.

I climbed back into the truck and turned to Lewis.

He wasn't in the cab.

I peered around the yard and spotted him relieving himself against the wheel of one of the trailers.

"HEY!" I shouted. "I asked you to watch the truck!"

"Sorry kid," Lewis called, "I was burstin'. I had three brews this mornin' waitin' for you." I looked around the cab and put my hand reassuringly onto the briefcase.

Still here, thank God. It's gonna be some trip, worryin' about this bloody thing all the time.

Lewis jumped up onto the cab step, clinging onto the wing mirror, and pushed his head through the open window. "Well?"

"Trailer number '13TA8582'."

"Right, I'll go and find it," he jumped down and strolled off in search of the trailer.

I started Big Edith and slowly moved across the huge concrete yard, scanning trailer numbers.

"Bert," shouted Lewis, "is this it?" He was pointing to one of the oldest-looking trailers in the yard.

Geez, I hope not.

I made my way over to him. *'13TA8582'* read the number etched onto the headboard of the trailer Lewis was standing next to.

Yep. This is our trailer.

"Scruffy old bastard innit?" Lewis was looking at the trailer with disgust.

"About right though."

No point in having a new trailer on Big Edith.

"To be honest," I added laughing, "this old trailer'll make Big Edith look smart!"

We hitched Big Edith to the trailer and did all the necessary checks. The guys in the office assured me that the trailer had a comprehensive check in their garage, which I believed, but there was no harm in checking again.

"Right, let's away to Dover our kid," I said to Lew, and we climbed back into the truck.

It wasn't long before we had to take a mandatory break, as set out in the HGV driving rules. By law, you couldn't drive for more than four and a half hours, at which time you needed to take a minimum of forty-five minutes uninterrupted break. It worked out quite well, because Lewis needed another wee and we were both Hank Marvin[1].

We sat down to enjoy the rubbery egg and wooden chips we had bought in the services – for a mere eight pounds sixty-nine each – when Lewis asked, "Have you got a map of Europe?"

"No I haven't," I replied, "but that's a good idea – we'd better buy one."

"Sod that! We'll use this one," he lifted his jumper slightly to reveal a brand new Philips map of Europe.

"Where didya get that from?"

"I got it while you were tellin' the bloke on the counter what thievin' buggers they were."

"I'm surprised nobody saw you take it."

"What? I'm not! Have a look at 'em - I've never seen so many dozy pillocks!"

We hastily finished our meal and made our way out of

---

[1] Starving

the service station to the truck. I was half expecting a hand on my shoulder any minute, but to my relief we got back to the truck without being accosted by security.

Once on the road again, we weaved our way back to the A1 heading south, then onto the A14 past Cambridge, and we flew down the M11 towards the M25.

"Hey, look," said Lewis, "that's Duxford Airfield innit? You know, where we went to that air show on the way to Dougal Arse's Auntie in Kent."

"Yeah, and that means we're still miles away from Dover." Just as I spoke, an unholy noise came from the engine compartment. I knew only too well what that was.

"What's that?" Lewis turned to look at me.

"Exhaust, must've blown hole in it! We'll have to get that fixed. Bloody China, my arse! We haven't even got out the country yet!"

"Hello, Douglas?" We had stopped at Tilbury services to ring Dougal Arse and tell him about the problem with Big Edith.

"How's that 'appened?" He enquired. He had an annoying knack of asking stupid questions.

"How d'you think?" I replied. "Bloody old age."

"Won't it get there and back?" Douglas asked. "It'll only be a bit noisy – just turn the radio up."

"Don't talk bollocks," I snapped at him.

"Only jokin', I'll ring ERF and try to book it in somewhere. Ring me back in five minutes."

We had a smoke to pass the time and phoned Douglas again.

"Nearest dealer to you is Canterbury," said Douglas, "that's the best I can do, but they can't do it until tomorrow mornin' anyway, so you'll have to stop at Margaret's tonight and get a later ferry tomorrow."

"Well?" Lew asked me as soon as I got off the phone.

"We have to take it to Canterbury to get it fixed, and

they can't do it until tomorrow. So, we're goin' to Kent for the night."

"Kent?"

"You were just talkin' about Dougal Arse's Auntie, weren't you? We can stay there tonight."

"You can sod off!" Lewis looked horrified.

"What d'you mean?" I asked, laughing.

"You know - Manky Margaret!"

We both burst out laughing, because Douglas's Auntie was a bit eccentric. She had chickens wandering all over the yard, even in the house, about five dogs (at the last count) that spent most of their day trying to catch rats, and to cap it all off she had pigs in the front garden. Other than that though, Margaret's house was alright.

About three and a half hours later, we arrived in a little village outside Canterbury. I parked the truck in a lay-by and walked down to the house with our bags.

Without hesitation, we walked into the house and went to the front room. Margaret never locked the front door. She reasoned that she had nothing worth pinching.

'And anyway, people are nice down here, not like those hooligans in Manchester.'

There was no use arguing with her, she was probably right anyway.

Margaret was about ninety years old, very sprightly, but her eyesight was terrible. She was a marvellous woman and she still had all of her marbles.

She had once owned a retirement home, but about fifteen years ago, she sold it and had a house built. Some of her patients went with her, saying they couldn't stay without Margaret. So she ended up looking after them until they passed away. The funny thing was that the oldest resident was about ten years younger than Margaret.

As we entered the front room, Margaret shouted, "I say! Who is it?"

"It's Jack and Lewis," I called.

"Ooh hello," replied Margaret enthusiastically, "you haven't brought that blessed awful Douglas with you, have you?"

"No, it's just us."

"Ooh, you must be hungry, do you want something to eat?"

"No," we replied in unison.

"We had summat to eat on the way," Lewis told her.

Every time Margaret and food were mentioned in the same sentence, it conjured up memories of the story she told us about one of her patients, Henry. Apparently, he used to leave his monstrous stools in the toilet pan, surviving every attempt to flush them. So Margaret would have to take the bread knife and chop them up.

She regaled us with this story on one of our first visits whilst making sandwiches. Needless to say, anybody who visited after that tried to avoid dining there if they could – just in case she had used the bread knife.

The Docks of Dover

It was six o'clock the next morning when I gave Lewis a shake and told him to get out of bed.

"What are we gettin' up at this time for?"

"So we don't have to have any food Margaret's made. If we're lucky, she won't be up yet. I'll go and check the truck over while you get ready." I whispered, picking up the briefcase and heading out of the bedroom. "Oh, and don't forget my bag," I added, popping my head back around the door.

Ten minutes later, I got back to the house and went around to the back door.

"-going cold!" I could hear Margaret saying over the clattering of dishes. I stopped for a minute to listen.

"Honestly Margaret. Er – I don't – I don't want any breakfast. I'm alright, thank you." Lewis was grumbling.

"You must eat it!" Margaret shouted, her shrill voice startling the chickens wandering around my feet. "You can't just waste good food like that!"

"Give it to Jack then."

"Jack doesn't want any breakfast. His stomach's upset worrying about driving to Denmark. But he said you always eat breakfast, and if you don't you'll be in a bad mood all day." There was silence for a few seconds. "That's why I've also done you an extra egg," chirped Margaret.

I walked through the door to see Lewis sat at the table, a look of apprehension on his face as he stared down at the plate of food.

"What's up Lew? Is it that good that you don't know where to start?" I laughed.

He looked up with a scowl and mouthed, "You bastard!"

"Come on, get it down you, we haven't time to mess about," I told him, still laughing.

"Help me!" Lewis whispered.

"Oh, all right," I said, walking to the door. I looked back and shouted "Margaret, come and see what's happenin' out in the back garden with your hens!"

"Ooh, what is it? It's not that blessed fox is it?" said Margaret, as she pushed past me to get to the back garden.

I nodded to Lewis, "Right, quick! Whip out the front and throw that to the pigs." Catching up to Margaret I added, "No, I was just thinkin' how happy they looked." It was obvious I was making up a pathetic excuse for getting her out of the kitchen, so Margaret went back into the house to carry on with her chores. "Good grief, look! Lew's finished his breakfast already. He must've been hungry, eh Margaret?"

"Ooh yes," she replied, "do you want another egg, Lewis?" Lew mumbled that he was full and left the kitchen as fast as he could.

We said our goodbyes to Margaret and Lewis gave his thanks to the pigs. As we walked back to the truck he said, "I'll get you back for that one, you rotten sod!"

I laughed, "Sorry, Lew. Couldn't resist! Did you eat any of it?"

"Did I buggery!"

"Well, you're alright then – stop whingin'," I said, smiling.

31

"You wait, I'll get you back."

"Right, let's see if she'll start."

Luckily she did, and we set off to Canterbury to get the truck fixed. We found the ERF dealership and parked up.

"I'll go in and sort 'em out, Lew. You drop the trailer."

I walked into the building marked 'Service' and approached the guy behind the counter.

"How do? Meadow Heights. We've got a trucked booked in to have a new silencer box fitted," I said.

"Ya wot, mate?" he said, with an awful southern twang.

I didn't have a lot of time for smug southerners so I repeated myself, emphasising each word as I did, hoping that this time the information would penetrate the thick skull surrounding his pea brain. "The company I work for is called Meadow Heights, and I believe that we have a tractor unit booked in to have a new silencer box fitted here this morning."

"Naw, mate," said the guy.

"What d'you mean no? I was told it was booked in."

"Yeah, it's booked in, but oi can't do anyfink wiv it 'til later on today," replied the chap, "all these lads are before you." I turned around to see four beer-bellied wagon drivers sitting behind me, smartly dressed in their company work uniforms, nodding and rolling their eyes at the guy on reception.

"But I'm supposed to be on the eleven o'clock ferry," I bleated.

"Ferry?" he asked, laughing. "Which one, the Woolwich ferry?" They all had a good giggle, until I explained where we were going.

"In that old bastard?" one of the beer-bellied wagon drivers asked.

"Yep, in that old bastard!"

"Well," the driver said, "you'd better let him go first. He needs all the luck he can get." At this, my opinion of the southerners increased, because they had all allowed me to jump the queue.

I pulled the truck into the workshop, picked up my briefcase, and left it in the capable hands of the mechanics. They said it wouldn't take long to do the repair, so Lewis and I asked where we could get a sandwich. One of the beer-bellied truck drivers told us where we could find a snack van nearby and we went in pursuit of some breakfast.

"They know all the butty stops them wagon drivers, don't they?" said Lewis, as we approached the van.

"Mornin' lads, what you 'avin'?" asked the old lady in the van, who looked to be about Maisie's age.

"Mornin', could we have two bacon on toast, and two teas please? I asked.

"Coffee for me," corrected Lew.

He's always gotta be difficult.

"And sausage on toast please, not bacon," he added.

"Ah, c'mon lads make your minds up, what's it to be?"

I looked at Lewis and shook my head.

"One bacon on toast, one sausage on toast, one tea, and one coffee please," I corrected. "So long as that's ok with you?" I glared at him.

"What? It's what I want!"

"Now, now boys," said the lady, looking at us sternly and busying herself with our order. "You lads aren't from 'round 'ere are you?" she said, changing the subject.

"No, we're from Oldham," Lewis replied.

"Oh, I know Oldham," she said. "Well, when I say I know Oldham, I mean I knew someone from Oldham."

"Oh."

"Right," we replied, trying to sound interested.

"Yes, a lovely man – he was in the army. Sugar?"

"Yeah please, I'll have two in the tea."

"Three for me please, in't coffee," said Lew. He turned to me and whispered, "In the army from Oldham? You don't think it's Pop, d'you?" He cleared his throat and asked, "Did he have a bad leg, this army bloke?"

"Sorry love, what was that?"

"Er – nothin'," replied Lewis, smiling at me.

"There you go lads," she said, placing our food and drink on the pristinely clean counter. "Four pounds twenty, please."

We ate our sandwiches as we made our way back to the ERF garage, laughing to each other. "She coulda been one of Pop's old birds, couldn't she? We'll have to quiz him when we get home!"

We walked back into reception and the guy behind the desk looked up. "All done."

"What, already?" I gasped.

"Yeah mate, already," he replied smugly, in that annoying twang.

I left Lew to sign for the work that had been done and went out to hitch Big Edith back up to our trailer.

I was in the middle of sorting the cab out when Lewis opened the passenger side door. I saw him hide something in between the side of the seat and the cab as he climbed in.

"What's that?"

"What?"

"That, you just shoved down the side of the seat?"

"Oh, it's some of them plastic seat covers they use when they service, you know? Stop seats gettin' full of shit, thought they might be handy if we get a bit dirty loadin' the trees."

"Good idea, our kid."

We pulled out of the big yard and set off towards the A2 and Dover.

I had no idea what to do once we arrived at the docks, so I decided to park up and see what the score was.

"You stay 'ere kid, and I'll go and find P&O's freight office," I said to Lewis, picking up the briefcase and leaving the truck.

I had to ask a few different people for directions, but eventually I found the right building. As I walked through the big, cumbersome entrance doors, I thought that if it had been the ticket office for car drivers, there would have been automatic doors.

Oh well, no point in wastin' money on a load of scruffy truck drivers.

It was decorated inside with whitewashed walls, posters of P&O ferry boats, warnings about the perils of rabies, and ferry timetables.

I approached the only vacant ticket window. "Hello, I've come to pick up a ticket for the Ostend crossing."

"Truck reg and company please," asked the girl.

She's a bit of alright.

"HNE 436T," I said, "and the name's Meadow Heights."

"Let me see," she said, punching her keyboard. "Yes, I have it here. Have you got your Customs note and weigh ticket?"

I stared at her and said, "Have I got my what?"

"Customs note and weigh ticket," the girl repeated, rolling her eyes skyward.

In my eyes, I had gone from looking like an international trucker, to looking like a right pillock.

"Er – no, I haven't done this before. I didn't know I needed anything."

"Well, I'm afraid you do," she said.

She pointed me in the direction of the customs building and left me to it. After half an hour of convincing the guys there that we were empty and trying to get to Denmark to pick up Christmas trees, I got the necessary note and returned to the truck.

"Sorted?" Lewis asked.

"Is it 'eck," I said, "we have to go and weigh the truck."

"What for?"

"It's so when each ship goes out they know how much weight's on board." I replied, putting the briefcase back on the bunk.

"Makes sense, I suppose, I know where the weighbridge is. I saw it when we were comin' in. I wondered why they had one."

He directed me over to the area where he thought the weighbridge was, and he was right.

"Well done, our Lew." I pulled the truck up onto the weighbridge and stopped next to the window of the cabin at the side of the bridge.

"Switch your engine off, please," said the guy behind the little window.

I turned the ignition off as requested.

Oh, I hope she starts up again.

I was paranoid about the truck not starting because, in the not too distant past, the truck would refuse to start for no apparent reason. Then it would rectify itself and behave. It had been behaving for a while now, so the odds of it stopping were narrowing every time we switched it off.

"Registration and trailer number please, mate," asked the guy in the window.

"HNE 436T and 13TA8582," I said.

"Are you loaded or empty?"

"Empty."

"And who are you sailing with?"

"P&O."

The guy finished typing on his keyboard in the one-fingered fashion that we men preferred.

"Right, there you go," he said, giving me our weigh ticket.

"Thank you," said Lewis and I, as the guy shut his little window.

I turned the key and the engine started up. A little wave of heat rushed through me.

"Right, let's try again," I said to Lewis.

Armed with the correct documentation, I returned to the P&O ticketing office. I didn't get to the same girl's window again. I spoke to a sour-faced old woman, who looked like she'd just had a box of lemons for her dinner. She loaded our information into her computer and gave me the necessary tickets for boarding.

I got back to the truck and looked for our lane number on the tickets. I then pulled Big Edith toward the quayside, and joined the queue for our lane. Looking around, it was pretty obvious that we had the oldest truck on the docks. I could see trucks from all over Europe; Spain, Germany, France, Italy, Ireland, Holland. You name it, they were here.

A Slow Boat to Belgium

Sitting in the truck waiting to be loaded onto the ferry, I decided to read through the tickets properly.

"Hey Lew, we get a free meal in the exclusive truck drivers' restaurant, and a free bed in a cabin!"

"Bollocks, I know what a lyin' sod you are!"

"No, it says right here, have a read yourself." I passed the tickets over to him.

"*Free meal and a bed,*'" read Lewis cynically, "I bet it's a bloody crisp butty and a deckchair."

"Well it should suit you then, tight sod!"

"What d'you mean?"

"What do I mean? When it's my turn to get meals you want the best, but when it's your turn we always end up with a bloody pork pie or summat."

"Yeah whatever," said Lewis. "Well, if that's true and I'm such a tight sod, you won't want one of these then."

"One o' what?"

"These!" Lewis exclaimed, producing with a flourish two plastic bags containing ERF truck T-shirts.

"You thievin' bugger!"

"What?" laughed Lewis, "I thought you got these free if you had a new exhaust fitted?"

"You'll get somethin' for free if they catch you! I knew they weren't seat covers that you stashed. Let's try one on though, they must be warmer than their bloody trucks." Lewis had a silly grin on his face as he tried his T-shirt on. "Anyway, what's going on? It's not like you nickin' stuff. I mean, at home you wouldn't even pinch a bottle of milk off the back of the milk float on the way to school, like the rest of us did."

"Dunno, I can't help it. I think it's somethin' to do with bein' away from home and thinkin' I won't get caught."

"Well you bloody well will, so pack it in." I told him.

"Hey up Bert, I think we're being boarded." I looked over. Ahead of us, the guys in the reflective jackets were motioning us forward.

"Bloody 'ell, squeeze 'em in, don't they? We've only just got enough room to get out the cab," I whinged. "Hey up! Watch your side, Lew! That Paddy comin' on behind us'll take your door off – you've seen the way them daft sods drive. Has he got a pig tucked under his arm?"

"I think the pig's drivin'," laughed Lewis.

"Well, they wouldn't be any worse than them." I opened my door and stepped down out of the truck. I shouted across to Lewis, "Have you got your cigs?"

"Yep."

"Good," I said, locking the door, "I can leave mine, then."

We made our way up the numerous flights of stairs to the upper decks. As we climbed, I was amazed at the number of trucks and cars that were aboard, and the army of men lashing the trucks down with chains to the huge shackles attached to the ship floor.

"Does that mean it's gonna be a bit rough?" Lewis asked.

"Sure no! Dey always do dat," said a little Irish guy who had overheard Lewis's query.

He was about five foot two with red hair and a set of

teeth that you wouldn't want in your pocket, never mind your mouth. His ears gave the impression that you could get Sky on the back of his head. He wore a kind of amazed expression, which looked to be perpetually etched on his face, like somebody had shocked him from behind.

"Do you do this trip regular, like?" I asked.

"To be sure oi do, boys," he said, "Oi'm between de Emerald Oile and Holland all de time," at which point he did that little intake of breath that some Irish people seemed to do to signify the end of their speech. It was a little like saying 'Out' when sending a radio message.

"So what's the crack with these cabins?" I asked.

"Well, you'd better go and get booked, 'cause dey go loike mad, you know."

"Where do we book one?"

"Well, go up to de information and you can book dem der."

"Thanks," said Lewis, "and by the way, what's your name?"

"Me name's Seamus."

"I'm Lewis and that's my brother, Jack." Lewis shook Seamus's hand.

"Sure, dat's an awful coincidence," Seamus said as he leaned over to shake mine.

"What is?"

"Me brodder knows somebody called Lewis at home. Sure, would you believe it?"

Lew and I looked at each other, tried to hide our grins, and headed toward information.

Once we had sorted our cabin out, I suggested that we get some food. At the entrance of the restaurant, we had to produce the portion of our tickets that gained us entry.

At first, I thought that we had come to the wrong place, because in my mind I had a vision of a scruffy little old transport cafe, the likes of which you get in England.

But we hadn't. The tables were set out with pink tablecloths, white linen placemats, candles, and gleaming silver cutlery. There was a maître d' on the door and inside were smartly dressed waiters and waitresses. Looking around, I was beginning to think that perhaps we should have dressed for dinner, or at least put on Lewis's new T-shirts.

The restaurant was quite full already, with a steady trickle of drivers coming in behind us. I wondered if it would be big enough to accommodate everyone. Our dining companions were a strange bunch. Some were sporting big handle bar moustaches, some had long beards, and others were wearing leather waistcoats with chains dangling from pockets or button holes. If I didn't know better, I would have thought they were bikers. Some guys even had wooden clogs on! We asked one of the guys why they wore them, and they said that they had always worn them and found them very comfortable. It didn't look that way to me, but who was I to argue?

We also spotted Seamus, but we were safe – he was happily ensconced with a table full of his countrymen, no doubt telling them about the amazing coincidence earlier.

There were all sorts of exotic-looking people in there; Spanish, Turkish, Greek, Welsh! But one thing was for sure, the place was full, and to be honest it looked like feeding time at Broadmoor Prison.

We had been informed by another passenger that there were English crews and Belgian crews, and today we were sailing under a Belgian crew. When I asked which the best were, we were informed that they were very similar, because the English crews were ignorant sods, and the Belgian crews were rubbish cooks. If you ordered a steak with the Belgian crew, you were advised to ask for it well done and not medium, because it'll have eaten your chips before it got to the table.

"Bloody 'ell, we get menus! Look at that," Lew shoved the menu under my nose.

"Fuckin' 'ell really? Bit posh in here, kid. Starters, main, dessert? And coffee? It's like a proper restaurant! Right," I said, perusing the menu, "well I'm havin' minestrone soup to start-"

"Salmon on croot? What the fuck's that?"

"It's fish, you lemon!"

"I know it's fish, but what's on croot? Does it mean salmon's on plate?"

"No, I think it's got pastry 'round it."

"Eugh! Salmon pie! Don't think so, I'm not havin' that! I'm havin' a steak, I don't give a fuck. We never get steak at home. And if we do, Maisie always burns it!"

We took the other passenger's advice and had a three course meal of minestrone soup (with extra bread for Lewis, the greedy bugger), sirloin steak, well done (but not really), and chips. To finish, strawberry cheesecake, all washed down with a couple of beers and a coffee.

"Well, I tell you what our Bert," Lewis said, as he leaned forward to fart and light a cigarette on the candle. "You can't fault that! Well I can, my steak could've been done for a bit longer, but hey – free meal!"

"Yeah, look at 'em out there queuein' at that shitty takeaway, while we sit in here. Just nice."

"Aye, I know," he said. "I seen a few of them tryna get in here, but the boss waiter just fucked 'em off."

"It'll be alright if we get treated as well over the water, won't it? Not like England, they treat you like scum if you drive a truck. It's nice to have it the other way 'round for a change," I added.

"Yeah," Lew flicked ash off his cigarette.

"Hey up, looks like your mate's on his way over."

"Who's that then?" he looked around. "Bloody 'ell, it's Seamus! If he comes over, I'm gonna fire him off."

"Hello der lads!"

"Alreet Seamus?" Lew replied.

Two-faced sod.

"Me and de boys were just tinkin', you know. Have you

got any road tax?" Seamus asked.

"Road tax?"

"Yeah."

"What, British road tax?" I asked.

"No, not dat shoite, de foreign stuff."

"Foreign stuff?"

"Yeah," said Seamus, "foreign stuff."

"Er, no."

"Well," Seamus continued, "der's a little kiosk just before you get out of de docks, on de left hand soide… well, oi tink it's de left," he thought for a minute. "Yeah, dat's roit, 'cause it's de opposite one to dat," and he held up his right leg.

"We didn't know you had to have different tax," I said, smiling over at Lewis.

"Ah, sure you do," said Seamus. "If the pollas stop you and you haven't got de tax, sure dey'll trow you straight in de clink."

"Thanks, Seamus. We'd have been locked up for sure if we were stopped."

"Ah, sure you would," Seamus said. "And buy de way, did you boys say you were going up tru northern Germany?"

"Yeah."

"Well, a bit of advoice der, boys, watch out for de Turkish drivers. Most of 'em are all roit, but der's a lot of arseholes up der on very little wages, and dey're bad enough to drag you out of your beds of a noite, slit your troats, and pinch all your monies."

"Are you takin' the piss?" Lew asked.

"Sure, are we fuck!" said another Irish guy who had popped up behind Seamus's shoulder.

"Sure, you froightened me to fuckin' death, you Patrick! Dis is Patrick, boys," said Seamus.

"Hi Patrick," we said.

"Hello der, boys," said Patrick. "Are we going playing de machines or what Seamus, or are you going to talk loike an old fisherwoman all noight?"

"No, we're away. See you later boys," said Seamus, walking away as Patrick waved.

"Aye, see you later lads," said Lewis.

"He's alright, your mate, isn't he?" I said.

"He's not me mate," he said brusquely.

"Could've fooled me." I started walking toward the stairway for the cabins.

"Let's go and have a look 'round duty-free, shall we?"

"Aye, all right," I agreed, "but don't be buyin' anythin' 'til later. It's about a four-hour crossing you know – oh, and don't bloody pinch anythin' either!"

"Would I?" Lewis laughed.

"They'll throw you overboard if they catch you."

We had a quick wander around duty-free, where there were plenty of cheap beer and cigarette brands of which we had never heard of. We decided that we were going to get a good selection later, just before the ferry docked.

"Right, I'm off for a kip. You comin'?"

"Aye," said Lew, "I need a crap anyway."

"You can have a crap up here, in one of these public toilets. You're not comin' down stinkin' our cabin out! You'll get us thrown off!"

"They'll throw us off if I have one up here, 'cause I stink. Anyway, there'll be nowt to read up here."

"There'll be nowt to read down in the cabin."

"There will," Lew lifted his pullover. "This." He produced a copy of the *Daily Sport*, which he had just liberated from duty-free.

I shook my head and said, "All right, but no wankin'."

When we arrived at cabin we found two sets of bunk beds with clean, white, cotton sheets, and a thick woollen blanket.

"Well, look at these, Lew. They're better than our beds at home!" I remarked.

"Yeah! Well, I'm bubblin'," Lewis replied.

"Keep the door shut!" I called, "I'm gettin' in bed."

The cabins must have been located very close to the engine room, because I could hear it rhythmically going about its business, driving the huge blades propelling us towards Belgium. With all the noise of the engine, it might have been annoying, but in contrast it was quite soothing, sending me off to sleep.

Just as I began to drop off, Lewis appeared and started to inform me of his 'good crap', but I just told him to make sure the door was shut, because I didn't want to be smelling it.

"Oh you'll be alright," Lewis said, "it's one of them fancy doors that won't let water in or out, you know, like they get on submarines, so it's not gonna let a fart out." He paused for a minute. "Have you got undressed?" he asked me.

"Yeah."

"What for?"

"You can't get in these nice beds with all your clothes on, you scruffy sod, so get undressed and get in properly."

"All right," Lewis said reluctantly. He got undressed, dragged himself up on the top bunk and crawled under the covers. "Hey, they're alright these beds, aren't they Bert?" I didn't answer. "Bert," Lewis said quietly.

"What?" I mumbled.

"What country are we going to first?"

"Belgium."

"Then where?"

"Holland, Germany and Denmark."

"Bloody 'ell!" Lewis said. "We should be able to get a shag somewhere out o' that lot."

On that note, we both dropped off for a well-deserved bit of shuteye.

BANG, BANG, BANG!

"Half an hour to docking!"

BANG, BANG, BANG!

"Half an hour to docking!" shouted the crewman as he made his way around the cabins.

We had been well away in the land of nod. I switched the light on to reveal that two more drivers had arrived in the cabin while we were asleep. Looking at them, I assumed they were Dutch because I noticed two pairs of clogs on the floor. The guys were lying on top of the beds fully clothed.

Scruffy buggers, no respect.

I gave Lewis a tap – he could sleep through a bloody bomb blast. When he woke, I pointed to our guests.

"Who are them two?" he inquired in a loud voice. "They better not've nicked 'owt."

I glanced over anxiously at where we had left our bags. Luckily, the briefcase was still there. Turning back to Lewis, I said, "Shhh," not wanting to wake them from their slumber. "Let's have a quick wash and go and get the duty-free. Keep your eye on the bags and that briefcase." I picked up my clothes and headed for the en-suite facility.

As I opened the door, Lewis's theory on submarine doors hit me full on in the nostrils. I started to retch.

"Just do what Pop says," whispered Lewis, laughing, "take deep breaths and it'll soon be gone." After a couple of swear words about his arse, I finally went into the bathroom.

After a short while, I came out and informed Lewis that it didn't smell anymore. "Are them two buggers dead?" I motioned toward the late arrivals.

"Dunno, let's just get goin'."

"Aren't you havin' a wash?"

"No," said Lewis, moving to the door, "'m alright."

When we got outside, I grabbed his arm. "What's up wi' you? Why you in such hurry to get out?"

"Nothing's up, I'm alright."

"Hold on a minute, you haven't half-inched² somethin'

off those two tulip chewers, have you?"

"Have I 'eck, you cheeky sod!" said Lewis defensively. "I'll tell you in duty-free, come on."

"Hang on," I said, "talkin' 'bout nickin' stuff, I better check this briefcase."

"Why? It's still locked up, innit?"

"Yeah, but you never know."

"Oh, so they're gonna unlock the briefcase – with no keys – pinch our tickets, and then lock it up – again with no keys – and get in bed, are they? Stop being so bloody paranoid and let's get goin'."

He had a point.

We got to duty-free with about ten minutes to spare, so we whizzed around with our baskets. We picked up eight hundred cigarettes of varying brands, eight bottles of wine, two bottles of whisky, and two packs of Grolsch.

"That'll do 'til we get to Germany," I joked to the pimply Belgian guy on the checkout. I might as well have asked him if I could shag his Grandma, because he didn't understand a word I was saying.

"Drivers, please return to your vehicles. The ship will be docking in five minutes." The request came over the tannoy and was repeated in at least two other languages.

"C'mon Lew, we'd better get back to Big Edith."

"What's the rush? There's loads of trucks, it'll take 'em ages to unload us all."

"Yeah I know, but we're right at the front, so we'll be one o' the first ones off!"

"Oh yeah, well I'm not rushin' down t'stairs with this lot, I'll go arse over tit!"

"There's no other way down."

"'Course there is, there's a lift," he said cockily, "in fact, there's two."

"Oh aye, smart arse, where?"

"Just follow me our kid, I'll show you." He led the way

---

[2] Pinched

to where the lifts were.

"How the bloody 'ell did you spot these?"

"Stick with me, our kid," Lewis replied smugly.

We joined the queue and saw that it was made up of mostly older and disabled people waiting for the lift.

"We're never gonna get in this lift Lew, let's just go down the stairs!"

The lift on the left opened with a *'ding!'*, and Lewis saw his opportunity. As two wheelchair-bound people were ushered into the lift, he squeezed past them carrying the packs of Grolsch with the cigarettes balancing on top. The two carers stopped and looked scornfully at Lewis occupying the lift.

Lewis smiled at them welcomingly, as though he were the lift operator.

"Come on, Bert!" he shouted.

I looked at the queue, who were all staring at me and Lewis.

Oh, bugger it.

I ducked my head and squeezed past them all, trying not to bang my four duty-free carrier bags full of wine and whisky on them all, mumbling "Sorry... sorry..."

When I got to Lewis I didn't turn around, I just stared at the back wall of the lift.

This is one of them moments when I just want a hole to appear in the floor and swallow me up.

I heard the lift doors close behind me and glanced sideways to see Lewis looking at me.

"What?" he laughed.

I got into the truck while Lewis passed up the goodies, and I stacked them under the bunk and in any other available orifices. "I can't believe you just did that."

"Oh, stop whingin'. We're 'ere now, aren't we?" I shook my head.

Bloody unbelievable.

Lewis climbed in the other side of the truck while I shut my eyes and, hopefully, turned the ignition.

Start, you old bastard.

She fired up like a young 'un, and I breathed a sigh of relief.

"Hey up, Bert! Look, the front door's goin' down – we'll be off in a foreign country soon," said Lewis excitedly.

"Never mind that, what was all that about when you were tryna get out o' that cabin a bit lively?"

"Oh, er… I thought you'd forgotten about that."

"Well, I haven't," I replied.

"Well, when you booked that cabin, did they know what our truck number was?" he asked.

"Course they did, why? Tell me what you've done."

"D'you know how you said I had to get undressed to get in that bed?"

"Yeah, so what you sayin', that you didn't?"

"No, I did," replied Lewis. "But, I mustn't have wiped my arse properly, 'cause there was a bloody big skidder on the sheets when I got up! That's why we had to piss off before that knocker-upper came back, 'cause he might've noticed!"

I shook my head in disgust. "I wouldn't worry about it, we'll just blame them two Dutch guys or whatever the scruffy bleeders were that rolled up in our cabin."

"Yeah, sod 'em," Lewis said. We both started laughing.

Beer Time

I started to move the truck forward under the instruction of the guys in the reflective coats. They were shepherding all the vehicles off the ferry as fast and as safely as possible so they could get loaded up again with the queues of waiting freight and cars to make the return trip to Dover. It was dark outside, and as usual, things had a habit of looking more intimidating in the dark, especially new, unknown places.

We moved slowly forward, two and three abreast with other trucks, to the gaping hole in the front of the ferry, or it might have been the rear. Then we stopped and waited for the boys in reflective jackets to indicate that it was our turn to descend the ramp onto foreign soil.

"This is us, Lew," I said as one of the guys beckoned us onto the ramp. I slowly moved the truck forward and off onto the dockside. "Well, we're in a different country now, kid!"

"Aye," Lewis said, "How different, though? D'you think it'll be better over here, or what?"

"Dunno, but I know one thing, I'm not goin' drivin' 'round this time o' night in a country I've never been to, and on the wrong side of the road as well. Tell you what, we'll see what the score is with this tax and see if we can park up, check in to a hotel and find some action."

"Oh aye, sounds just nice to me. But didn't you say we have to be up in Denmark by Tuesday?"

"Yeah, but sod that! I fancy a look 'round here."

I pulled the truck over to the side of the roadway out of the way of the other disembarking vehicles, while we got our bearings and sorted the cab out a little.

"You can't move in here for cigs and beer!"

"Nowt wrong with that," laughed Lewis.

"Where did your mate say this tax kiosk was?"

"Near the exit to the docks, and he's not me mate."

"I dunno, he liked you." I pouted my lips, wiggled my eyebrows and shook my head in a camp fashion.

"Naff off," Lewis replied, "A gay paddy? Don't think so."

Suddenly, there was a blast of a truck air-horn and an Irish-registered truck powered past us.

"There he goes," I said. "Give him a wave!" But Lewis just laughed and put two fingers up.

We waited for the other trucks and cars to vacate the ship before we set off in search of the tax kiosk. We found it quite easily, given that Lewis's mate didn't know his left from his right. I went into the building and, surprisingly enough, I was out within ten minutes.

"That was quick!" Lewis said.

"Oh aye, they never seem to mess about takin' money off you, no matter where you are."

"What's the crack, then?"

"Well, it's a fiver a day, and that enables us to drive in any countries on this sheet," I passed the piece of paper over.

"How many days have you bought?"

"Seven," I replied. "So let's hope we're back by then!"

"Well, we're alright," Lewis was scanning the sheet. "It's got *Belgium, Holland, France-*' are we goin' through France?"

"No," I said, "not the way we're goin', but you never know. Hey, I wouldn't mind throwin' my bones on a nice French bit, anyway."

"I tell you what, it's right what Bill said about you," Lewis said. Then he did his best impersonation of Bill with his hands on his hips and a stern face. "*Shag a dead dog, your Jack.*'"

Bill was an old guy who worked in the yard at Meadow Heights on a part-time basis, and what Bill didn't know or hadn't done wasn't worth talking about.

"Bollocks," I said. "He said that about you."

"Naff off," he laughed. "*Germany, Sweden, Spain*' – oh, and *'Denmark,'*" he read, still looking at the list.

"We have to stick this in the window somehow," I held up a square, official-looking piece of card.

"What's that?"

"The tax disc. The guy in there said we have to display it in the window."

After much fiddling and many unsuccessful attempts to stick the document to the window with some dodgy-looking stuff out of Lewis's bag, we decided to wedge it in the corner of the windscreen with an old cigarette packet.

"That'll do. Sound," I said, "apparently, we can park anywhere on the left here, because that was the last ferry in at this dock until half eight tomorrow mornin'" I got out of the cab and walked around to Lewis' side. "Pass me bag down," I said, once I finished relieving myself against the passenger side wheel of the truck.

"Here. Oh, and d'you want this bloody old briefcase you've been carryin' 'round everywhere with you?"

"Oh, aye. I'll have to take that."

"Why? It's only got our tickets in it, hasn't it?"

"Just give it here and let's find a hotel."

"Alright, but hold on a minute, I need a gypsy's kiss[3] meself."

---

[3] Piss

52

"Bloody 'ell, that pipe of yours sees more daylight than some people."

"Whatever," laughed Lewis, "anyway, it's dark," he added sarcastically.

"Good job as well, they're not ready for that big bugger over here yet, kid. You'll get us locked up."

"Sod off," he laughed, trying to squirt a jet of urine on me.

"Behave, you scruffy bugger," I joked, jumping out of the way. "Anyway, there was an English driver in that tax kiosk thing. He told me that there's a good hotel just off the square in the centre of town, it's called the Marion."

"How do we get there then?" Lewis asked.

"It's over the bridge by some old sailin' ship," I said. "And I'll tell you what else he told me, trucks are banned from drivin' on the roads in Germany on Sundays, so if we don't go on the pop[4] here tonight, we'll only be sat at the Dutch/German border all day Sunday, scratchin' our tatties[5] and gettin' in trouble. At least this way we can have a nice drive up to the border tomorrow in the daylight, park up for the night, and be away again on Monday mornin'."

Walking out of the dock gates, I could see a huge, old, schooner-type sailing vessel. It looked like something out of the Spanish Armada, although the only comparison I could draw was from the pictures I'd seen in history lessons at school. I had never seen anything as grand and imposing as this old ship in my life.

"Bloody 'ell," I looked up in awe at the masts on the ship. "It might be a bit fancy for us 'round here."

"Why?" asked Lewis, "just 'cause they've got a bloody scrap boat at the end o' the road?"

We both burst out laughing and started to make our way over the bridge toward what we thought was the

---

[4] Alcohol
[5] Testicles

centre of town.

"Here Lew," I shouted, "let's whip across the road while the lights are on red."

"Hold on a minute," he said, gazing off the footbridge into Ostend Marina.

"What's up?" I was worried that he had dropped something in the water.

"Nowt. I'm just looking at these boats, some beauties, aren't there?"

"Oh, aye," I said, looking over at the numerous yachts and cruisers moored up in the marina. "But you'll never get on one, so stop wastin' valuable drinkin' time, and let's find this hotel."

"Aye, alright." He suddenly snapped out of his daydream.

As we crossed the busy dual carriageway between the marina and town centre, we were having trouble coming to terms with the traffic being on the wrong side of the road.

"Good job we're not drivin' tonight," said Lewis.

"I know, we're havin' a job walkin', never mind drivin'."

The words were no sooner out of my mouth when a car came to a screeching halt inches from my legs. Even though I knew it was my fault for looking the wrong way, I felt angry and humiliated. I spun around and shouted, "Fuck off! You-"

Ready to launch into a tirade of the best English swear words I knew, I stopped short when I noticed that the occupants were gorgeous women. They looked to be about our age, both brunette, and very smartly dressed.

I was gobsmacked. I moved out of the way, allowing the ladies and the rest of the accumulated traffic to go by.

There's nowt like them in Oldham! And if they're all like that 'round here, Lew and I are in for a good night!

"Did you see them two birds in that car, Lew?"

"What car?"

"That bugger, the one that nearly run me over just

now!"

"No, I was bonin'[6] all these pubs in, look at 'em!"

"Bloody 'ell," I said, looking down the street. "Are they all pubs?"

"Looks like it to me."

The street in question was the Rue Pierre Curie and with the amount of neon lights advertising beer attached to the buildings, it looked like a drinker's paradise.

"It must be a mile long!" exclaimed Lewis.

"'S alright," I said, "but you know what we've forgotten, don't you?"

"What?"

"We've got no foreign money."

"Oh aye, didn't think about that."

"We'll have to look for one of them Change de Bureau places."

"Think I saw one on the ferry."

"Well, see if you can see one here."

We walked along the Rue Pierre, scanning side to side.

"Here, is that one Bert?" Lew was pointing to a neon sign on a building in front of us, and as we got closer he read aloud, in his best foreign accent, "'Boo Ro De Change!' It's 'Bureau de Change', not Change de Bureau, you lemon."

"Well, I was nearly right," I said, walking through the glass door banging my bag and briefcase on the door frame. Lewis was following close behind, but there wasn't a lot of room inside. The guy behind the glass screen looked up as we bundled our way in, but he was now looking down at his desk and fumbling with bits of paper, acting as though we weren't there. He was middle-aged with a bald head atop and nicely trimmed hair to the sides, wearing heavy, black-framed spectacles. Eventually, he lifted his eyes to look at us with an enquiring look on his face and forced a smile.

"Alreet? Can we have, er…" I turned to Lew and

---

[6] Checking out

whispered, "what money do they use over here?"

He looked at me vacantly, shrugged his shoulders and said "Fucked if I know, Belgium money?"

Well, yeah, of course it's Belgium money, you nobhead.

I turned back to the teller. "Can I have a hundred pounds in er -" I paused whilst I thought and blurted out, "Belgium money, please?"

"One hundred pounds *Sterling* to Belgian *Francs*," he said clearly in flawless English.

"Aye – I mean, yes please," I replied, correcting myself.

The teller entered the amount into his computer and swiftly produced a receipt of the transaction. He then pointed to the different figures on the receipt and started to explain what they meant. I tried to look interested, but my mind drifted.

Yeah, yeah, yeah, just give us the money.

"Okay?" The teller asked, once he had finished explaining.

"Aye, sound that," I said.

He looked at me curiously.

Bloody 'ell, I'm gonna have to start speakin' properly over here.

"Yes, okay. Thank you," I replied with a smile.

The teller pulled open a drawer and took out a bundle of banknotes. He counted the correct amount, then scraped a few coins from various compartments within the drawer and placed them onto the little pile of banknotes. He then put the notes and coins into the hollowed-out portion of the counter below the security window, counting it out as he did so. Once he had finished, he busied himself with bits of paper again and carried on as though there was nobody there.

I scooped the money out of the hollow and put it in my front trouser pocket. I always put money and anything else important in there, because I thought I'd be able to feel a pickpocket trying to get in my front pocket. If I put stuff in my back or jacket pockets, I might not. That was my philosophy, and I was sticking to it.

"See you," I said, and we turned to leave. The teller didn't even look up. "Right, let's find a decent pub, I'm as dry as a nun's – what's Jupiler?" One of the neon signs had 'JUPILER' written vertically on it. "I've never heard o' that!"

"I've never heard of any o' these buggers," said Lewis. "Oh, apart from that one," and he pointed to a 'Guinness' sign. "Bloody Paddies get everywhere," he laughed.

We went into the bar with the familiar logo. "Bit dark, innit kid?"

"It is. D'you think they're still closed?"

"Either that or they haven't paid the electric bill."

We looked around the dimly lit room and I could see about five guys playing on a couple of pool tables, while two or three more were sitting on tall stools near the bar. About four women were dotted about, leaning on the walls here and there. All of the guys were dressed in leather and sporting mullet haircuts and moustaches.

"Are we in a Hells Angels bar or what?"

"Lew, looks a bit dodgy in here to me!"

"A bit? That's an understatement!"

The barman asked us what we would like to drink, albeit in Flemish, French, or Dutch – not that it would have mattered because we couldn't understand him anyway. So, feeling on edge I snapped at the barman, "Two pints of Guinness."

The barman asked in an enquiring tone, "Are you English?"

"Yeah. Why, is there a problem?" I growled, as all eyes in the bar fell on us.

"No problem," said the barman, stepping away, "it is just that we have no Guinness," he added, again in perfect English.

"Fuck's sake Bert, calm down. You'll get us killed," whispered Lewis. "Could we have two pints o' that Juniper stuff?"

"Jupiler?" replied the barman, correcting Lewis ever so

politely.

"Yeah, Jupiler please, two pints."

"No problem. But it will not be a pint, it will be in one of these glasses." He held up a continental beer glass for Lewis' approval.

"Sound that," Lewis nodded, eyeing the glass.

The barman was still looking at him for some sort of approval. He quickly realised that the barman hadn't understood his last remark, so he held up a thumb and said, "Yes, they're okay." The barman didn't hesitate this time and started to pull our first continental beer.

As the beers were being poured and skimmed, Lewis turned to me. "What you so edgy about? We could slap our way out of here, no problem. We took on more than this in Rochdale when you were caught tryna shag the landlord's wife in the Robin Hood. Alright, we got knocked about a bit, but we stood our own."

"Yeah, but we didn't have ten grand in a scruffy old briefcase in Rochdale, did we?" I said.

Lewis stared open-mouthed at me and gasped. "You what!"

"Two beers," said the barman, interrupting our conversation.

We gave our thanks and the barman put a small block of wood with a nail through it in front of us. He swiftly pushed a bar ticket for the drinks over the nail.

"That must be our slate."

"Never mind that," whispered Lewis, scanning the room more vigilantly now, "you tellin' me that you've got ten grand in that peaty[7] old briefcase?"

"Yep," I said, half smiling, "so keep your eyes open."

"You're a rum bugger, you. What's it for, anyway?"

"What d'you think? To pay for the trees. They're Danish, y'know, not Red Indians. They want cash, not a bag of shiny marbles and half a dozen bottles o' bloody

---

[7] Dirty

firewater."

"I know that," laughed Lewis, "but I thought you'd just send a cheque when we got home."

"What? Would you let two numb-nuts like us roll in your yard, load over a thousand trees, and take 'em out of the country without payin'?"

"No, I suppose not," Lewis took a swig of his brew. "I tell you what though, beer's alright."

"It is, in't it?" I drained my glass. "Think we'll have another." I put my empty glass on the bar and said to the barman, "Two more please," holding up two fingers and pointing at the beer glasses.

The barman responded with a knowing nod and started to pull more beers. Lewis watched as he scraped the froth off the top of the beers with a spatula and gently allowed a drop more into each glass from the pump. He then put a circular paper doily onto the stem of the glass so it nestled to catch any spillage. I could see that he was quite taken with this show of professional bar work.

God, that's different from how Jean Travis pulls us a pint in The Red Rose.

Lewis turned to me and said, "They don't half bugger about here, Jean would've had us a pint on the bar in seconds."

"Ah well, you greedy sod, you're alright now, 'cause he's here."

The barman duly arrived, placed two more beers in front of us, and another ticket on the nail.

"'Scuse me," Lewis said to the barman just before he moved away into his corner again.

"Yes?"

"D'you know where the Hotel Marion is?"

"Here in Ostend?" the barman asked.

No, on bloody Mars.

"Yes, in Ostend," said Lewis.

"I have not heard of it," he said. Then he shouted something over to the living dead playing pool. The response was frightening, because each and every one of the Hells Angels descended on the bar around us.

The biggest, ugliest one asked, in the most perfect English, "Can I help you at all?" He reminded me of the posh one in *Gremlins*.

"Yeah," said Lewis. My grip tightened on the handle of the briefcase. "D'you know where the Hotel Marion is, please?"

"Yes," he said, and gave us directions. From the sound of it, it wasn't very far away.

All the other Hells Angels turned out to be a pretty decent bunch as they sat, talked, and had a drink with us. So, after a few more drinks, we left the bar and went hunting for the Marion.

"I tell you what Lewis, you can never tell what people are like by lookin' at them, can you? I would've put money on that lot being wrong'uns."

"I know, but they came and sat with us, din't they? Even bought us a few drinks – really kind."

"Yeah well, that's why I couldn't believe it when I saw you put a couple of our bills on their nail, you tight get," I laughed.

"I didn't think you'd seen that," he chuckled.

"Good job they didn't!"

French Girls

"*'Hotel Marion,'*" read Lewis, "this can't be it, can it? It just looks like a pub."

"Aye, it does look like a bar, doesn't it?" I corrected, because we were on the continent now, and they didn't do pubs.

"We've followed the right directions, haven't we?"

"Yeah! So it must be this place. Let's go in and see anyway." I pushed the door open and squeezed through to the bar with my bag and briefcase.

The grey-haired man behind it looked at us expectantly.

"Is this a hotel?" I asked.

"Yes," he replied rather sternly, looking us up and down.

"Have you got two single rooms for the night, please?"

"Go through that door to reception," he gestured to his right.

We went through a varnished pine door, into a rather narrow corridor with a reception desk at the end. It was about three feet long, with a lift-up portion at one end to allow access, a phone, and one of those little bells with a plunger on top to operate it. I couldn't resist.

"Where is she, then?" I expected to be greeted by a

female receptionist. I struck the bell with the palm of my hand and in my poshest voice called, "I say, you peasants! We need service here!"

My hand was coming down for the second strike, when the chap behind the bar appeared through a door at the back of the reception counter. Unable to stop myself, *'ting!'* went the bell as I struck the plunger.

The guy gave me a disapproving look and flicked open the reservation book he had pulled out from under the counter. I looked over at Lewis for some sort of approval for my latest stupid action, but he smiled mockingly, shaking his head.

"Two single rooms for one night?" said the guy.

"Yes please," I replied.

"Passports please."

"Passports?"

"Yes, I need to register them. It is the law."

I looked around for something to rest my briefcase on. I didn't want to open it on the counter, it was so small, he would've easily seen it was full of cash. So I crouched down with my back to reception and opened the two inset locks with the little key.

If a would-be thief wanted to get into the briefcase, the two pathetic locks wouldn't have posed much of a problem. But at least they offered a sense of security. I opened it just enough to extract the passports.

"Here we are." I closed the briefcase and gave the passports to Lewis, who handed them over to the receptionist. He immediately started to scribble the information on them into a big book.

Lewis turned away from the counter and gestured for me to do the same. "What you gonna do with that?" he asked, nodding his head at the briefcase.

"I dunno," I replied honestly, "I hadn't given it a thought."

"Well, I don't fancy havin' it with us all night. See if he has a safe."

"Rooms 103 and 104," the guy said, causing us to turn around. "They are on the first floor." He placed two keys on the counter in front of us. They had those huge, flat plastic fobs attached displaying the name and address of the hotel. "Breakfast is between seven and ten o'clock tomorrow and you vacate the rooms by twelve noon."

"That's alright, we'll be gone before then anyway," I said.

"What 'bout that?" Lewis nodded at the briefcase as I put the passports back.

"Oh yeah, have you got a safe?"

"A safe?" asked the guy, looking at us strangely.

"For this," I held up the briefcase.

"Ah. Yes, no problem. We have a good vault," he said, holding out his hand to take the briefcase.

I reluctantly handed it over. "Will it be safe?"

"Yes, of course," came the reply, accompanied by a look of disgust at me. Perhaps he thought that the last remark displayed an obvious lack of trust in him.

Realising that I had upset his feelings, I said "Sorry," and looked at him for some sign of forgiveness. I hadn't been questioning his honesty – it was just one of those silly remarks you make when you hand ten grand over to a complete stranger.

"I will put this in the vault now." He turned around and disappeared through the door he had so magically appeared from earlier.

I turned to Lewis with a worried look.

"Be reet," he said. We left to go up the stairs and find our rooms, negotiating our way up the narrow staircase to the first floor.

"Which room d'you want?" I held out the keys.

"Not arsed, kid."

"Here." I gave him the key to 104. I went into my room closing the door behind me.

The room was nice enough. It had an en suite bathroom, double bed, television, tea and coffee making facilities, telephone, and trouser press.

This'll do nicely.

The phone started to ring with a strange sort of trill. I had never heard it before, which only added to the mystery of who the caller may be. I shuddered, hoping it wasn't the guy at reception telling me that the briefcase had gone missing.

"Hello?" I said into the mouthpiece.

"You asshole!" Lewis did his best Arnold Schwarzenegger impression. Every time he mimicked a foreigner, no matter where they were from, he always ended up sounding like Arnie.

"You're the bloody arsehole," I laughed, "I wondered who the hell it was."

"Hey these rooms are alright, aren't they Bert?"

"They are. Tell you what, let's have a quick shower, shit, and shave, and go and get somethin' to eat, eh?"

"Oh aye," Lewis agreed, "see you down at the bar in twenty minutes."

"Alright." I put the phone down.

When I entered the bar area I could see Lewis was already sat there cradling a beer.

We didn't scrub up too badly, even if I did say so myself. We were both over six feet tall. I was twenty-three years old and Lewis was seventeen. We had fairly good physiques, and I thought we were quite good-looking. Given these desirable attributes, we never had much trouble attracting the opposite sex.

"Have you got me one of them, Lew?"

"Aye, he's just scrapin' froth off it," he motioned his head in the direction of the barman, who incidentally was not the one who checked us in earlier. This one was in his mid-twenties and shorter in stature, with a little bit of a paunch.

I sat waiting for my drink and I noticed that the back

wall of the bar area, instead of having optics hanging off it, had an elaborate pigeon-hole type timber framework. Each one of the pigeon-holes had a bottle in it. I roughly counted up and across, estimating that there must have been over a hundred bottles in the middle section alone, not even counting the sides, which were constructed in a stair-like fashion up against the middle section.

The barman arrived with my drink and pulled the receipt over the nail. I pointed towards the back of the bar. "'Scuse me, what's all that lot?"

Turning to look, the barman replied, "They are a selection of beers from all over the world."

"Bloody 'ell!" exclaimed Lewis, "how many have you got there?"

"We have one hundred and fifty, and a lot of them are strong Belgian beers. They range from four percent volume up to twenty-five percent."

"Twenty-five percent? Gee, you wouldn't want a session on them, would you?" joked Lewis. "D'you sell them?"

"Yes, we have at least six of each of the beers you can see in stock in the cellar, we also have these," he walked over to the corner and lifted the lid on a big chest freezer.

"What's in there?" I asked.

"Schnapps, we have sixty different flavours."

"No wonder that English guy told you 'bout this place, he must've been a right pisshead!"

"D'you serve food in here?" I enquired.

"No I'm sorry, we don't," he replied.

"Can you recommend anywhere?"

"What type of restaurant do you want?"

"Oh… er – I dunno. Indian? Is there an Indian round here?"

"No, I don't know of an Indian restaurant in the whole of Ostend," the barman replied apologetically.

"Well, is there a…" I thought for a second, "Chinese?"

"Oh aye," said Lewis, no doubt thinking of spring rolls

and spare ribs. "Chinky chinee, that'll do for me!" he rhymed. I was surprised that he wasn't drooling.

"Yes, the Jasmine Garden is in the main square."

"Right, that'll do us," I said, and drained my glass. "Come on, Lewis."

"We'll see you in a bit," Lewis said to the barman. "When we get back we'll have some of them fancy bottles o' beer."

"Aye, we'll be ready for a good drink then." I paid our bill and Lewis started laughing.

"You'd better knock a longer nail through our block later, kid!"

The restaurant was excellent. We had a good meal and decided to go back to the hotel and try some of those beers.

"You can't beat Chinese, can you?" Lewis mused as we made our way back to the hotel.

"No, you can't our kid. But I tell you what, we would've been a bit knackered if they didn't have the menus in English as well as Belgian."

"You're right, couldn't understand a bloody word – it's all 'dink' and 'donk' and stuff like that over here, innit?"

"You're a bloody donk."

"What d'you mean?"

"What do I mean? You, askin' that Chinese waitress if she was 'number one brow-job' and if she 'rove you rong time'." I mimicked his dodgy Chinese accent.

"She didn't understand," he laughed. "Anyway, I could do with gettin' a bit of work for this big bastard while I'm here," he grabbed at his crotch.

"Well, be careful where you put it," I pushed open the door into the hotel bar, "you might get it chopped off!"

The bar was busier now than it had been earlier.

This is more like it.

We managed to secure a couple of seats at the bar.

"Good meal?" enquired the barman.

"Oh aye, spot on," I said, "thanks for tellin' us about it."

"That is okay."

"By the way, I'm Jack and this is me brother, Lewis."

"My name is Gustav, but most people call me Gus."

"Right then Gus, let's sample a couple o' these bottles."

"Which would you like?" he asked, making a sweeping motion with his hand toward the rack of bottles.

"Oh, I dunno. What d'you think, Lewis?"

"Dead easy, we'll start at the top and just keep workin' our way down 'til we're pissed!"

We both laughed and asked Gus to select some beers for us. We told him that we would trust his judgement, since we were spoiled for choice.

As we were talking, we remarked on the fact that everyone could speak very good English. We were very impressed, because in England we didn't know anyone who could speak another language. He explained that it was compulsory in schools in Belgium, and throughout most of northern Europe, to learn English as a second language. This made me feel strangely sort of proud and special – people were taught *our* language.

Bloody good job, really!

We tried quite a few beers as the night went on, and Lewis's earlier advice about knocking a longer nail through our block wasn't looking like a bad idea now. When we were trying to decide whether to have another drink or go into town and check out some of the other bars, two girls came through the door and sat in one of the booths.

"I'll tell you what we'll do," said Lewis, "I'll go and have a gypsy's, and then we'll have a look around town."

"Aye, alright."

As Lewis disappeared into the toilet, one of the girls came over and stood next to me.

"Bonsoir, je voulais m'excuser – c'était moi qui a faille vous renverser tout á l'heure," she said.

I turned to look at her.

She was brunette, fair skinned, with the most amazing hazel eyes. She stood at around five foot six and had a lovely, slim figure. I guessed that she was about twenty-five years old. She wore a cream-coloured, silk, low-cut top and blue jeans, held up with a beige leather belt.

"Sorry?" I asked, not quite believing my luck.

"Ah! You are English? I think I owe you an apology," she said, with a hint of a sexy French accent.

"Apology?"

"Yes, I nearly ran into you earlier."

"Oh! Was that you?"

"Yes, I must apologise."

"No, no, it wasn't your fault. I should've been lookin' where I was goin' – I'm just a gormless pillock."

"Sorry?"

"Er – I'm just stupid. I mean – er – my name's Jack," I tried to change the subject.

She took my hand ever so softly and said, "I am Monique, very nice to meet you."

"D'you – er – d'you wanna – I mean, would you like a drink?" I asked, hoping my hand didn't feel sweaty.

"I am 'ere with my friend," she motioned toward the booth her friend was sat in.

"Well, I'm here with my brother, would it be ok if we joined you?"

"Yes, that would be nice," she smiled sweetly and walked back to her friend.

At that point, Lewis returned from the toilet. "Are we away, Bert?" he asked.

"Are we buggery," I gestured at Gus to come over. "See them two birds in that booth," I said, nodding my head in their direction and noticing that they were looking over at us.

"Yeah."

"Gus, do us a bottle of red wine and four glasses, will you?" I asked.

"Which one would you like?" asked Gus, pointing toward his selection.

"A strong 'un." I turned back to Lewis, "Well, that's them that nearly ran me over today."

"So, what's goin' on then?" he asked. Gus put a metal tray down on the bar with a bottle of red wine and four glasses on it.

"We, our Lew," I said, picking up the tray, "are goin' over with this bottle of knicker-loosenin' ointment and joinin' them."

When we arrived at the table, I introduced Lewis to Monique and she introduced her friend, Celine.

"Celine Dion, eh?" said Lewis.

Pillock.

"Sorry?" Celine asked, with a confused look on her face.

"Just ignore him," I said.

Celine had green eyes, slightly darker hair than Monique, and was about three or four years younger. She looked as though she could be a little bit shorter but it was difficult to tell with her sitting down. She had a petite build and was wearing a grey sweatshirt over blue jeans.

I could sense that they were two very different girls. Monique seemed level-headed and very classy, whereas Celine had class also, but I could sense the rebel underneath.

We talked about ourselves and the girls told us that they were cabin crew. They worked out of Ostend airport, and Monique explained that most of the flights they worked on were between Ostend and Frankfurt, carrying mainly businessmen and women.

Monique was originally from near Lyon in France, and had met Celine through the airline. Her parents had a farm in a place called Morestel and she had studied art at Lyon University. Celine was a local girl. She lived in the more affluent part of Ostend with her parents, who didn't approve of the work she did, saying that it was 'beneath her'. I thought that she probably only did the job to annoy them. When Monique was in Ostend, Celine's parents let her stay with them, 'because I might be a good influence on Celine,' Monique said.

We were getting on really well, so after about an hour Lewis asked the girls if they knew of any bars or clubs we could go to. To which Celine replied, "What a good idea, should we all go?"

Always the responsible one, I said, "Well, I dunno, we have to be away early in the mornin'."

"C'mon, you miserable sod, it'll be a laugh!"

Monique interrupted, "You two go, I will stay 'ere with Jack."

Lewis looked at me and smiled.

"Okay, Lewis," said Celine, jumping up, "you and I will go, and leave these two old people 'ere."

"You're dead right, love," said Lewis, and he leant over to me pretending to scratch his leg and whispered, "I told you I'd get some work for this!"

"Aye, well just remember what I said about it gettin' chopped off."

"Come on," said Celine, linking Lewis's arm.

Monique said something in French to Celine who replied in the same tongue, giggling and rubbing her head on Lewis's shoulder. I wondered if it was a similar sort of exchange as Lewis and I had.

"Hey," I called to Lewis, "don't be out all night."

"Alright, Mam!" Lewis replied sarcastically.

Eventually, the bar emptied and it was time to make a move. I thought I would push my luck and ask Monique if she fancied a nightcap in my room. Unfortunately, she politely declined, told me what a wonderful night she'd had, and again apologised for nearly running over me with her car.

"That's okay," I laughed, "you can nearly run over me anytime you like."

Then that uncomfortable moment came.

Should I try and kiss her?

As I was deliberating, Monique looked at me with those beautiful hazel eyes, leant forward, and kissed me on the lips for what seemed like forever. Pulling away, she softly bit my bottom lip. I felt a shiver run through my body and stood there in a trance as Monique made her way to the exit.

After a heartbeat, I came to my senses and chivalrously asked if I could walk her to the car.

"That would be nice," replied Monique.

"What about Celine? Don't you have to wait for her?" I asked as we strolled along.

"No, I often go 'ome first, it is not a problem."

We arrived at the car far too soon and once again, that uncomfortable moment reared its ugly head. As with the last, Monique soon dealt with it. She thanked me for a lovely evening, gave me a peck on the cheek, and got into her car.

No, no… I want you to kiss me again, like you did in the bar!

She drove away waving her arm out of the window, and I knew that I had just spent the evening in the company of a very special woman.

Lewis's Undies

Beep! Beep! Beep! Beep! Beep! Beep!

I stretched out my arm to turn off the alarm but I couldn't find it, so I had to raise my head off the pillow to switch it off.

"Half past bloody six." I mumbled as my head crashed down on the pillow.

I lay there with my eyes shut.

Sunday morning.

I should be at home, lyin' in bed and waitin' for Maisie to shout upstairs to let us know that breakfast's ready. Mmm, big Sunday breakfast. Bacon, egg, sausage, an—

Suddenly, my thoughts turned to the previous night.

Monique.

How lovely was Monique! What might've happened if she came upstairs with me?

Oh God! Lewis!

I opened my eyes.

I wonder if he's in bed.

I threw the covers back, swinging my legs around to sit on the side of the bed. I picked up the phone and followed the instructions for how to dial between rooms. The phone rang, again with that strange sort of tone.

No answer.

The phone rang and rang.

No reply.

"Sleep through a bloody bomb blast, him," I mumbled as I put the phone down.

I had a shower, got dressed, packed my bag, and tried Lewis's room again.

Still no answer.

So I decided to give him a knock.

"Lewis, Lewis," I said in a loud whisper, "get up, you lazy sod!"

There was no response.

"Have you got that bird in there?" I waited a minute for some sign of life. But nothing.

"I'm off for breakfast now, so come on, we have to get goin' soon."

I was getting annoyed.

I thumped the door a couple more times, then went down to breakfast.

The dining room was quite big. It had about twenty tables and, to my surprise, half of them were occupied. Up until now I had thought that there were only Lewis and I staying in the hotel.

It was a continental breakfast, you know – stale bread and jam.

'Bloody prison food,' Pop would call it. *'You can't beat a proper breakfast,'* he'd say.

I finished my second cup of coffee and got up to leave my crumb-covered table.

Where the hell is he?

I decided to ask the guy on reception to ring Lewis's room for me, just in case I had done it wrong earlier.

"There is no answer, sir," he said. I thought looked like the son of the older guy who checked us in.

"Okay, thank you." I said, making my way back to

Lewis's room.

Once I got to his door, tired of pussy-footing about, I gave three good, hard bangs on the door and called, "Get up, you lazy bastard! It's no joke now!"

There was still no response from inside the room.

I was getting really annoyed, but a part of me was slightly worried, so I went down to reception again and asked the man if he had a spare key for room 104, and if so, would he come up and open Lewis's room. He found the key and came back upstairs with me.

He opened the door to reveal an empty room, with a bed that hadn't been slept in.

Oh shit. Where the bloody hell is he?

All sorts of things started going through my mind.

He could have been run over on his way back to the hotel, or beaten up.

No, wait. Stop thinkin' the worst. He'll just be with that Celine somewhere, fast asleep.

But where?

I told the guy from reception that I would gather Lewis's stuff and meet him back downstairs.

"Okay," he said, probably sensing my distress.

"I'll fuckin' kill him." I started picking up Lewis's clothes and putting them in his bag.

As I systematically made my way across the room I came across his underpants on the floor. My mind flashed back to the situation with the bed sheets on the boat.

Bollocks to them, they can stay on the floor.

I collected the briefcase from reception and paid the bill for the rooms. As I opened the briefcase to check the contents, I half expected it to be empty. But to my relief, everything was still there. I left word on reception for Lewis, that if he were to show up he's to go straight to the truck and wait for me.

Loaded down with our bags, I walked through the

square and thought about what Maisie had said to us before we left. She was packing sandwiches and all sorts of other snacks for us to take. I had just told her that we didn't need anything, because we'd be stopping along the way and would buy our meals.

"You can't pay those prices all the time. Besides, you might not like the food," she said, fretting about our well-being. "Anyway, what do they eat in Denmark?"

"Probably reindeer," I sniggered.

"Oh, they don't do they? The cruel buggers."

"No, I'm only jokin', Mam. I think they'll just eat the same as us, so we'll be alright – we won't need to take any food."

"Well, I don't care. You're takin' it, and that's that." She made sure that we had enough food to last a good while, and put the bag near the door with our clothes. "If you haven't got it with you, you can't eat it, can you?"

But as we were leaving the house, she looked us both square in the face and said, "Make sure you look after each other."

"We're not going to bloody war, Mam," Lewis laughed.

"You know what I mean," she boomed, looking at Lewis disapprovingly for making fun of her serious request. "So you just think on, right?"

"Yeah, alright, Mam."

"Now, give us a kiss," she held her arms out laughing, knowing there would be no chance of that.

Only been out of the country one night, and I've lost the bugger.

I was walking over the footbridge near the marina when I heard a hiss.

"Bert, Bert." The hairs on the back of my neck stood up. I turned around to look for Lewis, but I couldn't see him. "No, over here," said Lewis's voice. I looked down over the bridge and saw him stood on the back of one of the fancy motorboats moored up in the marina.

"What the f- get off, before anybody sees you!" I shouted. I assumed that Lewis had just kipped[8] on the back of the boat, but I didn't really care. At the sight of him, I felt a great weight had been taken off my chest.

Celine came into view from behind Lewis and he shouted, "It's alright, it's her Dad's!"

You jammy bleeder.

"Well, come on then, we've gotta get goin'." I turned and started off toward the docks, where our truck was parked.

"Right, I'm comin' now." Lewis said his farewell to Celine and caught up with me as I got nearer to the truck.

"I wondered where the bloody hell you were this mornin'," I said, "I felt a right pillock bangin' on your door."

"Sorry, but I had to get me pipe serviced."

"Pipe serviced? I'll service the bugger," I grabbed his shoulders and playfully wrestled with him.

"Get off me, you bloody gorilla!" Lewis laughed. I did the usual checks around the truck, while Lewis decided to get changed. "Did you throw all me clothes in, Bert?"

"Yeah."

"Oh, you're a good 'un," he delved into his bag for his work clothes. I went to the front of the truck to check the oil and water. "Bert, where are me undies?"

"Probably in a skip now."

"What d'you mean?"

"I left 'em there. I wasn't pickin' them bloody things up. Anyway, what are you whinin' about? You've got a pair on."

"Yeah, I know," replied Lewis, "but these are for best, them were me work undies."

I jumped in the truck while Lewis finished off getting changed. Closing my eyes, I turned the key in the ignition.

Vroom!

---

[8] Slept

She was away.

I busied myself with filling in a tachograph disc, which were circular paper discs that you had to fill in with your name, the place you set off from, the truck registration, and the mileage. The disc would then be inserted into the tachograph unit incorporated in the dash. It was this disc that would be handed over if the police, or any other authority, were to stop you on your journey, because it recorded how you were driving. It was the law to fill one of these in every day, and then to keep hold of them afterwards.

Lewis clambered into the cab muttering, "Can't believe you left me undies."

"Shouldn'ta stopped out all night then."

"Ooh, alright Mam," he mocked.

I steered the truck through the big dock gates and out onto the highways of Belgium. As we passed the marina, I gave a couple of blasts on the air horns.

"Where is she, then?" I asked, as we both looked over at the boat that Lewis had slept on last night.

Celine didn't appear.

"Probably got back in bed," Lewis smiled, "'cause she'll be tired, you know."

"Yeah, you lucky sod!"

"You 'ad that Monique."

"I didn't."

"What d'you mean? You tellin' me that you didn't throw your bones on her?"

"No," I said, shaking my head.

"Bloody 'ell, why not?"

"Well… you know." I was unable to offer a reason for my passionless evening – not one that Lewis would understand, anyway.

"Well, I was reet up t'tatties," said Lewis, lighting a cigarette. "I tell you what, when we got on that boat, we were just messin' about at first, you know, kissin' an' that." He took a puff. "So I thought, in for a penny, in for a pound, and I whipped this bugger out. Well, she just went crazy."

"Ooh, you're just an old romantic, aren't you?" I said sarcastically.

"No, listen, some of the things she did-"

"I don't wanna know," I interrupted.

"Well, I can't believe you didn't nob that Monique," he said, leaning back in his seat and putting his feet up on the dashboard. "You must be losin' your touch, our kid."

I looked across and was about to say that I thought Monique was a bit special, and that it's not all about sex, but thought better of it. I turned back to the windscreen. "Fancy you endin' up on a boat, after I'd said you had no chance," changing the subject slightly.

"Aye, I couldn't believe it. When we came out of the disco I asked her if she wanted to come back to me room, but she said no. Then she just said that she had a better idea and dragged me down to the marina. When we got there she jumped on that boat, pulled a key out from underneath the anchor chain, and opened the cabin."

"What was it like inside?"

"I dunno really, we couldn't have the lights on in case somebody saw us. Celine said they might've flattened the batteries anyway, and then her dad would've known somebody had been on board."

"He must have some money. What does he do?"

"Buggered if I know, I didn't waste time talkin' about her Dad. I was busy with other things, if you know what I mean, kid?" He smiled and winked at me.

I knew what he meant, of course. "Get your map out. Let's see what road we need to be on."

Lewis pulled his new map out from under the seat and turned to the relevant page. "It looks like the A10… or is it the E40? They look like the same road to me."

"Aye, I've heard somethin' about that. The E number is a European route that goes through a few countries, and the A number is for the country you're in, I think. Summat like that anyway."

"Sounds like a lot of bollocks to me."

"Where we headin' for first?"

"Let me see," Lewis turned back to the map. "You wanna be headin' for Gent and then Antwerpen."

"Antwerpen? Don't you mean Antwerp?"

"Says Antwerpen here," replied Lewis dryly.

"It's strange, drivin' on this side of the road," I remarked, "you have to really think about what you're doin' at these junctions and roundabouts. Good job it's a Sunday and there in't much traffic about."

"Hey, you're doin' a good job, our Bert. I couldn't do it." That bolstered me slightly, and I drove with more confidence.

Aww, our Lew could say nice things… sometimes.

"It should be easier when we get on the motorway," I told him, "we'll just be goin' in a straight line."

As we drove through Ostend, I couldn't help but notice how nice it was. The road was lined with big, mature trees which were all nicely pruned. They weren't overhanging the road, or all different shapes and sizes like in England. Also, there weren't any leaves on the floor. Come to that, there were no fag ends or rubbish either.

I bet they've got a big, giant Maisie somewhere that they just let out at night to vacuum.

I started laughing.

We left the suburbs and entered the Belgian countryside. The fields were as flat as football pitches, and I could see for miles because the landscape wasn't interrupted by hills or undulations. There weren't even any trees in the fields, or hedges dividing them. I thought it was odd, but it was mainly arable land – perhaps the farmers had pulled them all out to make the fields bigger.

"It must be nice," Lewis said, after a lengthy period of driving with only our thoughts for company. I thought he'd fallen asleep.

"What's that, our kid? What's nice?"

"To have all this flatness. I mean, I've had a few scary moments in the tractor on those bloody hills at home. Imagine ploughin' one of them lovely fields, though!"

"Yeah, but knowin' you, you'd only get bored."

"I get bored at work anyway."

We were driving on the A10 motorway, heading towards Gent. The roads so far had been excellent, really well surfaced, with no potholes or roadworks, not even very much traffic.

Bloody marvellous.

I relaxed into my seat.

It'll do for me if it stays like this.

"Bloody 'ell, is that you?" Lewis was winding the window down, a look of disgust on his face as he scrunched up his nose.

"Aye, sorry kid, it's that winky-woo[9] we had last night."

"Sod all to do with that winky, you peaty-arsed bleeder."

"No, honestly, my ring-piece feels like a trainee glassblower's lips!"

"Better not have a smoke 'til that one clears," joked Lewis. "Let me know if you're gonna do any more of them, will you?" He wound the window back up. "I was thinkin', anyway, in't it funny, you endin' up with that Monique, after you said about wantin' to throw your bones on a French piece."

"Oh aye, bloody hilarious," I said sarcastically.

"Where are them sarnies that Maisie packed for us? I'm hank."

"Under the bunk. Anyway, you told her that we wouldn't need any."

He pulled a pack of sandwiches out. "So did you."

"She knows, that Maisie, dun't she? *'If you haven't got 'em, you can't eat 'em!'* " I mimicked.

"Well, she's right," he offered me a sandwich. I

---

[9] Chinese

declined, explaining that I had already eaten breakfast. "Well, I haven't."

"Whose fault is that, then?"

"I know. What did you have for breakfast, then? D'you get a full 'un?"

"Did I 'eck! It was continental-style – you know, coffee and baguettes."

"Aye, I slipped Celine a baguette this mornin' for her breakfast," Lewis said, and we both started laughing.

The Royal Mint

After a few hours of driving, we arrived at a place called Turnhout, which served as the customs post between Belgium and Holland. As we approached on the motorway, we had a choice of lanes to drive into, three set aside for cars and two for trucks. Both truck lanes had a sign above them, one with the letters 'TIR' printed on it, the other said 'TRANSIT'. Not having a clue what either meant, I opted to pull off altogether into the service area, which seemed to be one with the customs post.

"We might as well park up, Lewis, and go into the office to see what the score is."

"Alreet. D'you want me put a brew on?"

"Nah, we'll get a brew in there," I pointed towards the service station.

"Right, I'll try and have a tidy up in here. It's like a bloody pig sty!" he laughed.

Walking up to the customs office, it was clear that there was no one in there. I tried all the doors and looked in the windows. I didn't have any luck, so I returned to the truck, collected Lewis and the briefcase, and went into the services.

It was much like any service stop, apart from the fact

that the ladies behind the counter actually smiled as they asked us in Dutch what we would like.

"Two coffees, please," I replied, hoping she had just asked us what we wanted and not said 'Piss off, we're shut." But she asked in perfect English how we would like the coffees.

"Nowt flash, just a drop of acker bilk[10] and a couple o' lumps please," Lewis said.

"He means milk and sugar please," I told her, looking over at Lewis disapprovingly.

The lady was laughing to herself as she gave us our coffees. I reckon she probably thought that she could understand English, until we started speaking. We took some complimentary biscuits and went to find an empty table. There were a few other truckers in the place; some sat on their own, others in little groups, all of them probably taking the mandatory break required by law.

"I wonder what the score is with the customs here," I said.

"Maybe they don't bother on a Sunday – they just let you cart Bob Hope[11] wherever you want," laughed Lewis.

One of the guys from the table opposite us leaned forward and said in a thick Welsh accent, "Are you boys English?"

To which I replied, "Yeah, are you Scottish?"

"No, Welsh," he said, curiously.

"I'm only havin' a laugh, where 'bouts you from?"

"I'm from Swansea, and this boy's from Cardiff."

"Oh hiya, I'm Jack an' this is Lewis, me brother. We're from Oldham."

"I'm George, and this is Owen."

We acknowledged each other with nods and I asked, "Do you guys know what the score is with customs?"

"How do you mean?"

---

[10] Milk
[11] Dope/Drugs

"Well, I've just been to the customs buildin', and there in't anybody about."

"No, they don't do Sundays, boyo," said George.

"Well, how do we get a ticket, or whatever?"

Obviously, he didn't know what I was talking about, so he said, "I don't understand. You just need your T2 form, isn' it?"

Oh shit.

"What's a T2 form?"

"Well, it's the documentation for the load you're carryin' see?"

"But we aren't loaded."

"Well, that's okay then," George said.

The T2 form was the document you got at your place of loading, and as you pass through different customs, you surrender it to them so that they can monitor goods either entering or passing through their country. And seeing as we weren't loaded, we didn't have to wait until the morning to get a stamp.

George informed us that this border was a bit relaxed, but he had heard that the German and Danish borders were different. He couldn't tell us how though, having never been that far north himself.

We ended up talking to George and Owen for quite a while. They were carrying newly minted coins to Eindhoven airport to be air freighted to Nigeria. George worked for the haulage company driving the truck, and Owen went along as an escort from the mint, to oversee delivery to the airport.

"That sounds like a good job," Lewis said to Owen.

"Aye, not bad, but it's only once in a while we get over the water – we usually just go to airports in the UK."

"Here, do you lads want some of these?" Lewis asked, and he pulled a bloody great handful of biscuits out of his pocket, the ones that had previously been for sale on the counter. I stared at Lewis as he handed them over to our new Welsh friends. He looked back at me, shrugged his shoulders, and smiled.

"Don't you ever get worried about being hijacked?" I asked, turning back to the guys.

"Not really," replied Owen, chewing on one of Lewis's biscuits, "because what would a robber do with twenty-four tons of foreign coins see? He can hardly take them to the bank, can he?"

"No, I suppose not," I replied, feeling a little foolish.

When we had finished our coffee and biscuits, we said our goodbyes, returned to the truck, and set off for the German border.

"I tell you what, if there hadn't been a sign, you wouldn't know we were in Holland now, would you?"

"What d'you mean?"

"Well, everythin' still looks the same."

"What did you expect? Chippies and Holland's pie wagons everywhere?"

"No," I laughed, "I dunno what I expected really. I'm surprised at you though, givin' away your ill-gotten gains in there."

"What ill-gotten gains?"

"Them biscuits, you thievin' bugger."

"I thought they were free with the coffee," he laughed.

"Aye, two packets. Not bloody twenty-two."

"Yeah, well, I thought if I got collared[12] I could rope them two taffies in as well, and say they made me pinch 'em. They'd believe me, y'know, 'cause I've got one of them innocent faces, haven't I?" he said, fluttering his eyebrows at me.

"One of them arsehole faces, more like."

"Here, look, the language is different on the road signs, but really, they're still the same as in Belgium."

"How do you make that out?"

"'Cause we can't understand these bloody signs either," laughed Lewis.

---

[12] Caught

"No, you're right, our kid. If everybody didn't speak English, we'd be in a right mess."

The motorways were an absolute dream – straight as arrows, smooth, wide, and flat, with hardly any traffic either, just the same as it was in Belgium. "Hey Lew, did you know that Belgium is the only country in the world that has its whole motorway network lit up?"

"And?"

"And! Just thought you might be interested."

"Oh aye, very interestin' that, Bert," he said sarcastically.

"Piss off."

"What speed you doin'? Seems like we're hardly movin'."

"Fifty mile an hour, that's all you can do in trucks on motorways over here, not sixty like at home," I told him.

"Bloody 'ell, at this rate, we'll never get there!"

"'Course we will, stop whingin'."

"Get your foot down, and I'll dog out[13] for coppers."

"Oh, aye, what do the cop cars over here look like then?" I asked.

"Buggered if I know."

"Exactly, there could be one up our arse now, checking the speed, and we wouldn't even know."

"Hey, I tell you what, I haven't even seen a cop car at all while we've been drivin' over here, have you?"

"No, that's a point, in England you can't move for the buggers."

"Yeah, you're reet there Bert kid, so get your bloody foot down," he laughed.

After a few more hours of uneventful trucking through the boring Dutch landscape, we arrived at Venlo, the Dutch/German border and customs post. It looked a bit more business-like than the last border, but just like the Dutch border it had a service area with restaurant and

---

[13] Look out

toilet facilities. There was no point in trying to sort customs out until the morning because, as the guy told us in Belgium, trucks were banned on the roads in Germany all day on Sunday. So we decided to park up for our first night sleeping in the truck.

Pete the Paraffin Lamp

The truck parking area was quite empty, so we didn't have a problem finding a spot.

"Park over near them toilets," laughed Lewis, "'cause if I need an emergency Barry White[14] later on I won't have to run far with me hand over me arse."

It was getting quite dark now, so Lewis busied himself pulling the curtains around the windows of the truck.

Hotel Edith wasn't the nicest place to spend an evening. It was a single-bunk cab, approximately seven or eight feet door-to-door, and five or six feet front-to-back. The seats and bunk were upholstered in dark brown/beige fabric, somewhere between carpet and army fatigues. At roughly the same height, the engine cowling was set between the seats, which enabled Lewis to spread himself across it to try and sleep.

The engine cowling didn't afford any comfort, because it wasn't designed for sleeping on, it served to separate the engine from the inside of the cab. It also had the gearstick running up the side protruding above the cowling by at least six inches, which made getting comfortable rather

[14] Shite

difficult. But at least it had carpet on it.

The cab had four lights set into the ceiling at each corner, each one giving about as much light as an aging firefly. The bunk I had the pleasure of sleeping on was eighteen inches wide and seven feet long. It was really luxurious, made of a one-inch thick ply board sheet, with a four-inch deep piece of foam bonded to it. All finished in the same, lovely material as the seats. It was like sleeping on a spongy cheese grater. The cab was finished off with a set of curtains, which were attached to a swish rail that ran above all the windows.

Home.

"What are we doin' about snap[15]?" I asked, "'cause it looks like the services are shut."

"I'll get the stove out and warm a couple of tins of that soup up, the ones Maisie packed."

"Maisie strikes again, eh? Right, you get that on our kid, I'm off for a slash."

Stuart, our older brother, had kindly allowed us to borrow his camping stove, which ran off a gas bottle that we had stashed behind the seats. It was a compact little thing. It looked like a steel briefcase. When it was opened up it had two burner rings and a small grill below.

I got back, opened the truck door and the smell of tomato soup hit me straight in the face. I had to admit, it smelled lovely and I was so ready for it.

"Hey, that smells good."

"Does, dunnit? I've put some toast on as well, just nice with soup." He passed me a can of Grolsch lager. "Here, get one of them down your neck."

"Cheers kid, you make a good Maisie."

"Well, only fair innit? You do the drivin' and I'll do the Maisie-in'."

"Alright, but don't be bloody tuckin' me up in bed later on," I said, laughing.

---

[15] Food

Lewis tipped half the contents of the pan into a bowl and gave it to me, along with three of his lovingly-prepared slices of toast. Sitting in the truck cab, eating soup and toast, drinking beer, and being kept warm by a camping stove was not exactly The Ritz, but oddly enough, it had a homey feel about it.

After a few more beers and a bottle of wine – which, incidentally, we wouldn't have been able to open had Stuart not lent us his Swiss army knife along with his stove – we decided to retire and see what tomorrow had to offer.

"Bert."

"What?"

"Are you comfortable?"

"Oh aye, just nice."

"Well, I'm glad somebody is," he grumbled sarcastically, "'cause it's hard as iron on this engine cowl, and the gearstick is stickin' up me arse."

"Well, go and kip in the trailer then, there's bloody loads o' room in there," I farted and rolled over, hoping he'd shut up soon.

"Piss off. And you can knock that fartin' on the head as well. It's dangerous enough in here as it is with that gas bottle, never mind your arse."

"Sorry, kid. It must've been your tomato soup."

"Oh, an' if you have to get up in the night for a gypsy's, don't be standin' all over me."

"I'll just hang it over the edge here then, shall I?"

"You know what I mean. There's no bloody room in here."

"Alright, I'll be careful kid. Now shut up and get to sleep. Oh, and wake me up at about half six with tea and toast."

"Sod off," he yawned.

The next morning, it was rather cold when I woke up. I immediately felt sorry for Lewis, because he had to get dressed first and tidy away his bedding before we could fire the cooker up and get some warmth into the cab. I knew that it would be pointless to start the truck. It wouldn't generate any heat because the engine wouldn't get hot enough until we actually started moving.

Most modern trucks were equipped with night heaters, which ran off diesel out of the truck's fuel tank and worked independently of the truck's heating system. But ours was a bit of an antique in the trucking world and we had to make do with our own heater – Stuart's camping stove.

"Did you kip alright?" I asked, with genuine concern. I remembered him grumbling last night, and he didn't look too fresh right now.

"Did I fuck! I woke up when you crawled all over me when you went out for a piss. Then I couldn't get back to sleep because there was a bloody draught comin' up from the gearstick, so I got some of your clothes and stuffed them in the gap to block it up."

"Oh, thank you very much."

"Then," he continued, as if I hadn't spoken, "when I finally got off to sleep again, some bastard pulled up at the side of us with his bloody fridge motor runnin'."

"Well, I've had a really good kip," I said, smiling at Lewis.

"I don't fancy kippin' in here again, Bert. If we do, I think I'll have to get a lot more pop down me, 'cause last night it didn't seem so bad when I was Oliver Twist[16]."

"I know what you mean. But if we do, you can have the bunk and I'll kip on the cowling."

"No, you're alright kid. You need a decent sleep if you're drivin'. It's just me havin' a whinge, you know what I'm like in the mornin'."

"Yeah, you miserable sod," I laughed, "get that brew on."

---

[16] Pissed

We were interrupted by two loud bangs on the passenger door. Lewis and I looked at each other, wondering who it could be.

"Ignore them, it's probably somebody wantin' money for parkin' fees or summat," I said.

BANG. BANG.

They weren't going away.

"I'll just have a peep 'round the curtains," Lewis said. He pulled the curtains down enough at the top to see a man in his late thirties, unshaven and looking a bit dishevelled, dressed in scruffy jeans and a moth-eaten pullover. "Looks like a fuckin' paraffin[17] to me."

"Oh fuck him off, Lew."

Lewis pulled back the curtains again, wound the window down slightly and said, "Fuck off, you scroungin' bleeder."

"'Ow art', alreet?" said the paraffin in a broad Yorkshire accent.

"He sounds like a bloody Yorkie," said Lewis, turning back to me.

"What does he want?"

"A bloody wash, by the look of him," he faced the window again and said, a lot more politely, "what's the matter? You alright?"

"Well, I'm sorry to bother thee, I've got a puncture on't trailer, an' I pulled onto 'ard shodder. Nah I've managed to get ma'sen in't services wi' it, but when a wen' for't get wheel brace to change wheel, I couldn' fun it."

'Ard shodder? Fun it? Bloody 'ell, if they struggle to understand me and Lewis, they've got no chance with this pillock.

"So when I saw t'British plates on tha' motor, I thought I'd ask if I could borrow thee's."

"Have we got a wheel brace?" Lewis asked me. "He's got a puncture and his has gone missin'. At least, that's what I think he said. It's easier to understand Dutch than

---

[17] Tramp

Yorkie."

I got out of the truck to give assistance to our fellow countryman, even if he did sound like a bloody foreigner.

"Here y'are," I said, handing our wheel brace over to him.

"Cheers mate, I'll bring it reet back tha'nos."

"D'you need hand?"

"Oh, please, if tha' dun't mind."

"Yeah, no bother. I'm Jack, and t'other lad's Lewis, me brother."

"Ma name's Pete." he said, holding his hand out. "Pleased to meet thee."

I told Lewis I was going with Pete to help him change the wheel, as well as to keep an eye on our wheel brace, because he might've just buggered off with it.

"I'm supposed to be in Berlin by toneet," Pete said as we made our way through the truck park, which was a lot busier now than it had been when we arrived last night.

"How's it you're changin' your own wheel, anyway?" I asked. "I thought you would've had the German equivalent of ATS or someone to do it for you."

"Tha' must be jokin'. Our gaffer's that tight, he wouldn't gi' a door a bang, he's not payin' them extortionate prices. So, we've t'get full o'shit an' risk our lives by changin' 'em us sen."

"You've got a nice truck though," I eyed his brand new Volvo truck, one of the 'Swedish rubbish' trucks that Douglas had told me about. "I tell you what, Pete, I'll change your wheel, and you can have my truck."

"Oh aye, he looks after us wi' motors," Pete replied, "that's a bit of a fuckin' 'eap you're in though, in't it?"

Slightly annoyed at Pete's remark, I said, "Well, we can't all have new motors, can we?"

"No offence," he replied, probably sensing that he had upset me, "all I meant was that you'd think your gaffer would've sent you in somethin' a bit better, considering t'distance that tha's going. All I mean is, all gaffers are tight buggers."

"Aye, I know what you mean Pete, but it's the only truck we've got," I explained how we ended up on the trip in the first place.

"Bloody 'ell," said Pete, "well, I wish ya good luck, just be careful where tha parks up in Germany, 'cause there's been trouble wi' some Turks robbin' drivers as they sleep."

"Yeah, a guy on the ferry mentioned that. What's that all about then?"

"Well, apparently some Turkish drivers are only on abaat thirty paand a week, so they're meckin' t'wages up by robbin' other drivers. Sellin' drugs as well, but don't worry abaat it too much, most of em are good lads, an' they don't like these odd arseholes meckin' 'em look bad."

After we had finished changing Pete's wheel, we went back to our truck, collected Lewis and the briefcase, and made our way into the restaurant to get cleaned up and have some breakfast. Pete said it was his treat, and we weren't going to argue with that.

"Oh aye," I said, "I'll have bacon and egg."

"Tha' won't," said Pete, "they don't do bacon an' egg 'ere, all you get is continental type, tha' nos, a bit of a baguette wi' jam and butter."

We had a decent fill of the buffet breakfast, which consisted of various cereals, lots of different types of bread, and croissants with ham and cheese to go with them. Pete then took me into the customs building while Lewis went around the truck doing the necessary checks and preparing us for the next leg of the journey.

At German customs they asked me to fill in a form giving basic information such as truck registration, driver name, and so on. Oddly enough, I had to write down how many litres of fuel we had in the tank. Pete said this was relating to tax. Apparently, you were only allowed into Germany with two hundred litres of fuel. Any more, and you had to pay tax on it. He said that everybody lied on that part, but now and again they were known to check.

Fortunately for us, I didn't have to lie, because we needed diesel anyway.

I was quite impressed, because Pete had a conversation with the guy at customs – it sounded like he could speak better German than English. When I asked how he became so fluent, he told me that he had been stationed in Germany for eight years while he was in the army, so he picked up the language. According to him, it wasn't that difficult to learn, because it was very similar to English. I couldn't see it myself, but I took his word for it.

Pete said goodbye, asked me to pass on his goodbyes to Lewis, and walked off in the direction of his truck.

What a decent guy. For that matter, how good have all the other drivers been, offering help and advice.

Lewis was just finishing packing everything away. "Everythin' alreet, Lewis kid?"

"Aye, sound," he offered me a cigarette, "I've put you a tachograph in as well."

"Right, cheers," I reached down and turned the ignition.

Vroom!

She was away again.

A bit of a fuckin' heap 'eh? You cheeky Yorkshire bugger.

"It is Venlo here, in't it Bert? 'Cause that's what I put on the tacho disc for the departure location."

"Yeah sound that, Lew. We'd better get some diesel on the way out."

We pulled over to one of the numerous pumps allocated to trucks and Lewis got out to fill the tank while I went into the shop to pay.

"D'you want me to come in with you?" shouted Lewis, smiling.

"I don't, no."

Thieving bugger.

The cashier took my Barclaycard and put it on the

rolling machine which takes an impression of the details, which was a relief because I wasn't sure they would accept it outside the UK.

I got back to the truck, jumped in, and said to Lewis, "Right, get that stolen map out kid, and let's see what Germany has in store for us. Hey, d'you know what Pete was carryin'?"

"No, what?"

"Sausages."

"Sausages?"

"Aye, it's a right fiddle, apparently."

"How d'you mean?" asked Lewis.

"Well, Pete said that he picks up sausages in Holland, and they're packaged up as if they were produced in England, y'know, all English writin' and that. Then he takes his truck onto the ferry back to Dover and picks up fresh paperwork on the docks, 'cause then it looks like they're bein' exported out of the UK. He's off to Berlin now, with a load of 'British' sausages that were really made in Holland."

"What a bloody fiddle!"

"Aye, goes on all the time, Pete said, with all sorts of stuff, not just sausages."

"You dunno what goes on, do you?"

"You bloody don't, do you? Hey, try and get some decent music on that radio, will you?"

"It's all rubbish over here, I haven't recognised one tune yet – oh, apart from that bloody *Cliff Richard* one in Belgium."

"Put one of me tapes on, then."

"Bollocks, they're worse than the radio."

"You cheeky bleeder!"

"Well, what d'you want on?" Lewis began trawling through the tapes on the dashboard, "*Abba, Stylistics, Slade* – Chris de fuckin' Burgh! Who bought this? Is it one of Maisies?"

"Hey, he's alreet, is Chris!"

"*Carpenters*," Lewis continued looking through the tapes, "*Police, Supertramp -*"

"Oh aye, get *Supertramp* on."

"*Supertramp*? I've never heard of 'em. Is it Pete's band?"

I started laughing. "Just get it on."

As *Breakfast in America* blared out of the overhead speakers it started to get lighter and the traffic got heavier. It wasn't long before we were in the complicated motorway network around Essen and Dusseldorf.

The traffic was really busy, we were obviously caught up in the morning rush. Apparently, it was the industrial heartland of Germany, and during the war it produced all sorts of military hardware, so it was bombed quite regularly. It must have been an easy job to hit one of the buildings, because I had never seen so many factories all in one area. They went on for mile after mile.

We eventually left the smoky, miserable buildings of Essen and Dusseldorf behind. I complimented Lewis on his navigational skills, and we both celebrated with a Gitane cigarette, which were part of the selection we had purchased from duty-free on the ferry.

"Bloody 'ell," choked Lewis, after taking a pull, "these are strong buggers!"

"You're right, they are," I said, exhaling smoke, "what did you say they're called, Shitanes?"

"No, but they should be," laughed Lewis.

"I tell you what, if we keep smokin' these in here, we'll end up with a couple of bloody soot rings on the ceilin'!"

The motorway – or autobahn in German – was mainly concrete, and was full of dodgy repairs and pot holes, making the journey extremely bumpy and rough. They were in total contrast to the motorways in Belgium and Holland, which were constructed of tarmac and as smooth as Maisie's well-worn ironing board.

"Hey Lew, did you know that these motorways we're drivin' on are the ones Hitler had built just before the war?"

"You can tell, 'cause they're knackered!"

He wasn't wrong, of course. The roads were in a state of disrepair, the old concrete they were constructed of was finally crumbling away, but it was testimony to the guys who built them all that time ago that they had lasted this long.

"Mind you, if you think about it, when these were built they were probably the first motorways in Europe," Lewis said.

"Yeah well, they say that's how Hitler managed to get troops and that into other countries so fast, 'cause of this motorway network."

"Well, they're about buggered now – they want renewin'."

"Better go and dig Hitler up then," I laughed.

The German countryside wasn't flat like Holland and Belgium. It was more interesting with its rolling fields and pockets of forestry. The canals were also a lot wider, with huge working barges on them. They made our canal network in the UK seem quite pathetic. This trip was certainly an education for Lewis and I, because we thought our country was the best. Now we were realising that there were plenty of other good countries out there. As they say, travel broadens the mind. Well, it was certainly broadening ours.

Space Age Ablutions

"Right Lewis, we'll have to pull in at the next parkin' spot for a break. I can't believe it's been nearly four and half hours since we left Venlo."

"It's that traffic we got lumped up in, took some time to get out of that Duffle bag place."

"Dusseldorf," I corrected, laughing.

"Here we are Bert, two kilometres."

"Two kilometres what?"

"Parkin' place, two kilometres away."

"How d'you know that?"

"Just seen a sign that says *'Rastplatz, two kilometres'*, that means car park, so there won't be any services there."

"How d'you work that one out?"

"'Cause I've been takin' notice, haven't I?" he replied smugly, "And *'rastplatz'* is car park, and *'rasthof'* means services. Just stick with me, our kid."

He's right.

Well done Lew, you strike again.

Clever bugger.

We pulled off the autobahn into the parking area, which was empty apart from a red Toyota van, which seemed unoccupied. The parking area had a WC block in the middle of it, and it was so clean and free of graffiti that it looked as though it were new and had only been opened that morning.

"Right, I'm off for a Barry," Lewis announced.

"Aye, alright. I'll keep me eye on this lot, then I'll go when you come back."

"I'm surprised you need a Barry, 'cause after smellin' that one you dropped about half an hour ago I thought you'd already had one."

"Whatever." I set about lighting Stuart's camping stove to make a brew.

The passenger door opened again.

"Gimme some of that toilet paper Bert, just in case there in't any in there. Oh, and pass me that *Daily Sport* for summat to read."

"Hey- "

"I know, no wankin'."

As I was pouring the hot water into our mugs, Lewis returned from the toilet.

"Hey I tell you what, our Bert. I've never been in a toilet like that one," he said, putting the *Daily Sport* in my lap.

"Why, what's it like?"

"Just go and see for yourself."

"Right, I will." I picked up the paper and left the cab.

As I neared the toilet block I heard Lewis calling me. I knew what he was going to say, so I put two fingers up in his direction without turning around. I heard him laughing and the door slam shut.

When I got in the toilet block, I was amazed at how clean it was. All the walls had stainless steel panels about six feet high with white tiles above them. The floor had the same white tiles, which were all lovely and clean. The sinks and urinals were all stainless steel too, as were the toilet cubicles and pans within them.

But who keeps it so clean and fresh-smellin'?

I couldn't even tell that Lewis had been in here. There didn't seem to be any attendant or cleaner around.

If we had this toilet block at home, it'd probably be vandalised.

It's a shame, but it seemed that we had more than our fair share of halfwits in the UK.

After using the facilities, I looked around for a handle to flush, but there wasn't one. I looked on the floor and walls for a button or something, but I couldn't find anything.

Bloody 'ell! How'm I supposed to flush?

I went to open the door to see if there was a button outside the cubicle.

The toilet flushed – they were automatic! As I looked around again, I spotted the sensor on the wall. Even the sinks were automatic – I just had to put my hands near the taps and the water came out.

Bloody marvellous!

I got back to the truck and climbed in the driver's side.

"Well? Summat else them toilets, aren't they?"

"They aren't half," I agreed.

"Did you suss out[18] that flushin' carry on?"

"Not right away."

"No, me neither. I was just gonna piss off and leave it," he laughed, "but then it flushed when I went to the door. I thought, thank fuck for that."

"Aye, that's just how it got me. Bloody brilliant though, aren't they? Not like them dumps back home."

"It'd get smashed up at home."

I nodded in agreement and finished my tea and biscuits, kindly supplied by Lewis's liberation department.

---

[18] Work out

"Yeah, I Can Speak German Now!"

Lewis packed the stove away and I walked around the truck to make sure everything was ok. When I jumped back into Big Edith, Lewis handed me a lit Shitane. I looked at him half smiling and he glanced back with a big grin.

"Gotta smoke them sometime, Bert."

"Suppose so," I said, turning the key in the ignition.

Vroom!

I steered Big Edith out of the still deserted parking area, and waved goodbye to the space-age toilet block. The sun was shining through the cab windows so it felt quite warm, even though it was a crisp winter day outside.

"What d'you reckon?" Lewis said, eyeing the toilet block.

"About what?"

"That shithouse."

"What about it?"

"Well, there was no bugger about, so what if it isn't even supposed to be open yet, and they're havin' a grand openin' later today?"

"Oh aye, that'll go down well when they find out two scruffy English men have had a Barry White in there already."

"Yeah, I can imagine the Mayor, just about to cut the ribbon sayin', *'Fee-Fi-Fo-Fum, I smell the farts of an Englishman!'"* he sang.

We re-joined the autobahn and Lewis started to fiddle with the radio again, mainly because he was sick of listening to *'old bastard music'* i.e. my tapes.

"You'll not find 'owt," I told him, but just as I said that, an English-sounding voice came through the speakers. "Hey, well done kid."

"Whatever it's like, it can't be any worse than that squeakin' bugger, bloody crispy burp."

"*Chris de Burgh,*" I said, defending my musical taste. Mind you, even I had to agree that most of the songs on the album were crap. To be honest, I don't know why I bought it, but I wasn't going to tell Lewis that. Lewis had tuned us into BFBS, the British Forces Broadcasting Service. It was actually a really good station, and made us feel at home, even though it was broadcast out of an army base somewhere in Germany.

As we slowly but surely headed north it got to that time of day again, when we had to think about parking up for the night. We had been driving for nearly eight hours, and the maximum you were able to drive in any one day was nine, so we decided that we would stop at the next services we came across.

The services were in Westenholz on the E45, somewhere between Hannover and Hamburg.

"*'Four kilometres die rasthof,'*" said Lewis, showing off the bit of German he worked out as we had been travelling along, "that means services, you know!"

"I know, you told me," I reminded him, not really interested.

"Yeah, I can speak German now! *'Ausfahrt'* means exit-"

"Does it? I thought that was summat to do with your arse."

"No, honest, I think I could learn German pretty fast, you know."

"Well, let's see how good you are in here then," I pulled into a parking bay in the service area. "You can order us tea – ah no! I've just realised, we haven't got any German money!"

"And I'm bloody starvin'," Lewis complained.

"I know, I'm 'ank myself. We'll have to see if they take credit cards, should be easy enough to ask, seein' as I've got an interpreter with me," I looked over at him.

"Shuddup," he passed me the briefcase.

We walked up the steps and went through the entrance, scanning the services for a Bureau de Change. We couldn't see one, so we decided to go to the dining area.

It was waiter service so we took seats at an empty table. Looking around, it was quite smart.

Like a proper restaurant, not like our service stations back home.

Lewis and I must have looked to these people the way Pete had looked to us – a pair of scruffy buggers. We hadn't had a shave or a wash since Belgium.

It wasn't long before a smartly dressed chap came to our table and asked us in German what we would like to order. We asked if he spoke English and judging from the expression on his face, it was obvious he didn't.

"Go on then, Lewis, get two steak and chips ordered."

The waiter put a menu down in front of us both and wandered off to another table to take their order.

"I thought they were all supposed to speak English on the continent."

"Aye, Gus said they all learnt in school."

"Trust us to pick a waiter that used to peg[19] off a lot," laughed Lewis.

"I can't make head nor tail of this menu. I bet you can though, can't you?"

---

[19] Skip

"Naff off. Anyway, we don't even know if they'll take your card, do we?"

"Aye, we do. Look, there's a Visa logo on the back of the menu."

"Here I'll sort some snap out, just watch this – hoy!" he shouted to the waiter, who looked around at him rather disgustedly. He pointed to another waiter who was coming out of the kitchen with a plate of food. "Two," Lewis called, as he held up two fingers and pointed at the food the guy was carrying, "two of them for us," he swirled his finger around in our general direction.

"Ah, okay," said the German waiter.

"See? He spoke English all along."

"I don't believe you sometimes. What the bloody hell have you just ordered?"

"Sausage and mash."

"How d'you make that out?"

"Well, it looked like sausage and mash."

"You could hardly see the food he had on that plate."

"Oh, stop moanin' and get your ciggies out. And don't be givin' me one of them shitanes – we'll stink the restaurant out with them."

After about fifteen minutes, the waiter arrived at our table with the food Lewis had ordered. As he put the plates down, Lewis asked, "Can we have two beers, please?"

"Bitte?"

"I dunno, what kind of bitter is it?" asked Lewis. "It's not that shit we have at home, is it?"

"Wie bitte?" said the waiter, with a puzzled look on his face.

"Bloody right it's wee bitter," laughed Lewis, "you must've supped some yourself."

I picked the menu up, pointed to the beers, and held two fingers up. He got the message, and scurried away to get them – he couldn't get away fast enough.

"I hope he doesn't piss in our beer now, 'cause of you

teasin' him," I laughed, "anyway, *that* is definitely a sausage, but what this other stuff is, God only knows."

"Well, it looked like mash when it were on that other plate."

"It looks like shit on this plate."

"Shuddup and have a taste."

It had the texture of raw cabbage, but it was warm and carried a strange taste, unlike anything I had ever tasted before. I looked at Lewis and without saying a word, I knew what he was thinking.

"Well, sausage in't bad," I said, "it's not Wall's, but it'll do."

"I'm gonna make sausage butties with mine. When he comes back, see if you can get some more bread."

When the waiter returned with our beers, we immediately started to drain the glasses, and once he put the ticket for them down on the table I said, "Two more, please," gesturing at the empty glasses, "and some more bread," I pointed at the empty breadbasket.

"Yeah, and bring us a nail for our bitter bills," added Lewis.

"Wie bitte?" said the waiter.

"Oh don't start all that again," laughed Lewis, "just go and get the pop."

The waiter walked away looking even more confused than he did last time.

We had a few more drinks, paid the bill, and went back to the truck to get ready for bed. The truck area of the service stop had really filled up while we had been in the restaurant, and as we got back we had a bit of a shock.

We seemed to be surrounded by Turkish registered trucks. There were two on the driver's side, one behind us, and another one a couple of bays down.

We couldn't see anyone in the trucks, so we assumed that they were in the services getting something to eat. We got into Edith and I set the camping stove up while Lewis sorted out the curtains.

"What d'you think about them Turks?" asked Lewis.

"How d'you mean?"

"Well, two people have said that they're thievin' buggers, and we're surrounded by them," he said, looking worried.

"Well, what can we do? We can't move anywhere else, truck park's full. Anyway, Pete said most of 'em are alright, so stop worryin'," I told him.

"It's alright for you, you're up on that bunk - I'm down here. They'll get me soon as they open the door, and the bloody passenger side doesn't lock," concern etching his voice.

"Well, sleep t'other way 'round, they'll soon piss off when they smell your feet."

"Hey, it's no joke! I'm kippin' with the bread knife next to me."

I drifted off to sleep listening to Lewis chunnering[20] to himself.

"Bert, Bert, wake up," Lewis whispered.

"What is it?" I said, sitting up.

"It's them fuckin' Turks, they're all at the front of our truck. I bet the bastards are plannin' a raid on us. Where's that bloody bread knife?"

"What time is it?"

"Half three."

"Have you been up all night watchin' for them?"

"No, they just woke me up with their talkin'."

"Get back to sleep, you paranoid pillock, if they were gonna do 'owt, they would've done it by now," I reassured him.

"I wish they'd piss off," he said, peeping at them through a nick in the curtains.

"Go and offer them a shitane each – they'll soon piss

---

[20] Muttering

off," I said, rolling over and trying to get back to sleep.

"Bert, Bert!"

"Fuck's sake! What now? I'll tell them to drag you out meself in a minute, so I can get some kip."

"No, look. They're goin'."

"Oh, good," I closed my eyes again, but opened them almost immediately and sat up. "Where's that bloody briefcase?"

"Ooh, who's paranoid now then? It's here under the bunk, where you always stash it."

After Lewis was sure the last of the Turks had disappeared, he settled down to get some sleep.

Lost

When morning arrived, I went through the motions of readying the truck for another day's journey, while Lewis put the brew on and made some toast. Everything seemed fine in and outside the truck. It looked like Lewis's Turkish friends hadn't tampered with it in any way.

We started off down the autobahn towards Hamburg, and Lewis got his map out and planned our route north.

"We should be dinin' in Denmark tonight, Lewis kid."

"What, in a hotel?"

"Oh, aye."

"Good, 'cause I don't think I could do another night in here – draughty, old bastard."

As we neared Hamburg, Lewis told me what junction we needed to be swapping autobahns on so we could carry on up to Kiel, and ultimately into Denmark.

Somewhere along the way, though, we got lost.

"I don't think we're on the right motorway," Lewis said.

"Well, you're the one reading the map."

"You must've took a wrong exit, 'cause according to this, we're goin' in the opposite direction to what we should be."

"Well, I'm only goin' where you told me," I snapped.

"Hey, don't get bastardy with me, I'm just tellin' you we're goin' the wrong way. Would you prefer I didn't say 'owt and just let you keep drivin' 'til we got to Berlin?"

"No, you're right. Sorry Lew. Considerin' how far we've come and this is the first cock-up, you haven't done badly kid."

"Well pull off at the next exit, whip round the roundabout, and go back the other way."

It was a considerable distance before we came across an *'ausfahrt'*, as Lewis liked to call them now he was in Germany. I pulled off the autobahn onto the slip, but at the bottom it merged into a normal country road. I looked across to see if there was another slip road on the other side, one that would enable us to re-join the autobahn and go back the way we had come. There wasn't.

"Oh, shit. How we gonna get back on the other side, now? I thought it'd be like home, with a roundabout or somethin'," I admitted.

We travelled on for two or three miles down the road until we came to a housing estate, which was the first opportunity we had to turn around. Driving in, I noticed a guy leaning on the side of a Suzuki four-wheel drive car talking to the girl occupant. I stopped alongside them. The guy gave me a strange look, which I would have done in his position – two scruffy-looking buggers in a bloody great foreign articulated truck, driving through what looked like the German equivalent of *Brookside*.

"D'you speak English?" I asked.

And with one of the most welcoming smiles I had ever seen, the guy replied, "Yes."

"Oh, good, 'cause we're lost and we need to get on the autobahn for Hamburg."

"I will give you directions," he said. He then explained how to get back on the autobahn to Hamburg.

I thanked the guy and his girlfriend and pulled the truck down to a street junction. I executed a perfect turn in the road manoeuvre – the kind that only articulated vehicles could do. Our new German friend was clearly impressed – he held both thumbs in the air as we passed. I pulled the air horns and waved as we drove past them.

We followed his directions and managed to get back to the autobahn. Now all we needed to do was make sure we took the right exit for Hamburg.

I was driving more carefully now, studying the signs, when Lewis called, "Hey, look who's at the side of us!"

I looked over and saw that it was the German guy in the Suzuki with his girlfriend driving. He was gesturing for us to follow him. He took us through the various lane switches to get us on the right track, and when he was sure we were alright he put his arm out of the window of the jeep with his thumb up – then they sped away up the autobahn.

"I hope nobody calls Germans to me, Lewis, 'cause you couldn't fault that guy, could you?"

"No, you couldn't our kid, so let's celebrate him with a shitane, eh?"

"Aye, why not?"

Forgery

Driving through Hamburg on the autobahn was quite a sight. Everywhere I looked, all I could see were steel shipping containers. It looked like every container in the world was here, they were even stacked right up to the side of the autobahn. As we travelled past them, we found ourselves on an elevated section which enabled us to look down at some of the big container ships that were docked up. I was ready to bet the traffic behind us thought we were about to break down, we were going so slowly.

When we came down off the elevated section, we saw signs for a tunnel. It was the tunnel which ran under the river Elb, and the sign informed us we were one kilometre away.

"I hope you don't have to pay a toll," I said, "'cause we ain't got no money."

"Well, that Kennedy tunnel in Belgium was free, and that was pretty big," Lewis replied.

On approach, the Elb tunnel was quite impressive. It was made up of three tunnels, each one wider than the Dartford tunnel, so you didn't get that awful, cramped, claustrophobic feeling you got in those narrower tunnels. The system in place had two tunnels running to cope with whichever was the busiest side, for instance the southbound would have two tunnels for the morning and northbound would have two for the evening. As we emerged out of the other side, it was evident that there wasn't a toll charge, and that had been a much bigger tunnel than Dartford, which you had to pay to use.

"There's always somebody with their hand in your pocket at home," Lewis remarked.

We headed north out of Hamburg passing the signs for Kiel, which was the last city in Germany on our route.

"Next stop, Denmark."

"Next stop, diesel," I said, "we're a bit low."

Fuel and food never seemed to be far away on the autobahns, and it wasn't long before we were pulling in to fill up.

"I'll come in with you when you've filled up."

"You'll have to watch our gear and that bloody briefcase, I'll be glad to get rid of that money – it's a pain in the arse."

"I'll have it."

"You know what I mean."

"I tell you what then, I'll go in. I've signed for your card before."

"When?"

"T'other week, when we went Light of Bengal."

"You said you'd paid for that!"

"Yeah, I did… with your card."

"How d'you manage that, then?"

"Well, remember when you said that you'd pay on your card, and I could give you the cash back?"

"Yeah… and?"

"And, you left your card and went for a gypsies. So, while you were away, the waiter came round and took a print of your card, so I signed for it." He was smiling.

"Hey, you're a rum bugger you. Here's me thinkin' you'd bought me a meal, and all the time I've paid for it meself! You owe me a tenner!"

"Yeah no problem, our kid," he laughed, "so, shall I go in and sign for the diesel then?"

"You might as well, why don't you add forgery to your list as well?" I shouted after him as he walked in to pay.

While I was waiting for Lewis to return, I had a good look around the truck to make sure everything was still ok. I climbed back in, expecting to see Lewis sat there, but he still hadn't come out. I was wondering if he'd been caught out with my card or-

Oh no, I hope he hasn't been nickin' stuff again.

I looked up and he came out of the door, carrying something under his arm.

"Here, have a look at that," he said, climbing into the truck and tossing a magazine at me.

"What is it?"

"Wank mag."

"What've you bought one of them for? Or have you nicked it?"

"No, I had to buy it. But just look in it, its proper porn, and they're not on the top shelf or 'owt, like in Ken Tatt's shop at home. They just have 'em on the counter next to the bloody wine gums."

As I pulled away, I looked over at the payment kiosk, half expecting somebody to come running out, shouting *'THIEF!'* at us in German.

He must've actually bought that magazine.

I glanced over and he was eagerly pawing his way through it, saying things like *'Ooh, look at shoulder boulders on this one!'*

Then I realised, if he *had* bought it, he must have paid for it on my card.

"Hey, did you get that mag on my Visa?"

"Yeah, how else d'you think I paid for it?"

"It'll show up on my Visa bill as porno," I whinged.

"Will it bollocks!"

"Well, what does it say on the receipt?"

"It says *'Three hundred litres of diesel and one wank mag,'*" laughed Lewis, pretending to read the receipt.

"No, I'm bein' serious."

"It just says diesel and another word that looks like *'zeitung'* or summat – it dun't say porn anyway, unless *'zeitung'* means porn."

For the next hour, I didn't feel like speaking to Lew a lot. I was too busy being pissed off at the fact that he had bought porn on my card, but as we made our way steadily north toward the Danish border, my mind turned to other matters. It had started to snow.

"Bloody 'ell, we could do without this," I moaned.

"Aye, they're not reet good in snow, these buggers, are they?"

"We'll be alright," I hoped, "just have to take our time, that's all."

"Aye, you're a good likkle driver, Bert."

The snow was falling steadily, hitting the windscreen without melting into droplets.

"Next junction's Padborg, the Danish border."

"Another customs, kid?"

"Aye, I wonder what this one'll be like."

I could see the cars ahead of us approaching a booth in the distance. However, the Danish border signs were clear and precise, so we followed the route it suggested for trucks, leaving the motorway earlier than the cars did.

"Urddy Gurddy!"

We followed the signs for a few miles down a country road until we reached the customs compound. It had an electronic barrier across the entrance with a pole at the side. There was a speaker on it, two buttons, and a credit card slot. It was lucky that Lewis was with me, because everything was on his side. It was all set up for left-hand drive vehicles.

"What you supposed to do here, then?" Lewis asked.

"Dunno, try pressin' one of them buttons," I suggested. He pressed a button and shouted into the speaker.

"Urddy gurddy!"

"Shuddup, you pillock," I laughed.

"Well, I dunno what to do, do I?"

"Well, you don't shout fuckin' *'urddy gurddy'* to 'em! Just press it again and say *'hello'* or summat."

"Hello? 'Elloooo? Is anybody there?" Lewis called, as though he was at a séance.

"Stop pissin' about, it's bloody serious, is this."

"Well, you fuckin' do it then!"

"'Ave ya got trouble, like?" said a guy who appeared at the side of Lewis' door.

While we had been trying to work out the barrier, we didn't notice that another truck had pulled up behind us, and its driver had got out to give us some assistance.

"How d'you get the barrier up?" Lewis asked.

"Did a card not pop oot the slot?" he asked in a Geordie accent.

"No."

"Well, just keep ya finger on that bottom button an' they'll see ya on camera, an' they'll send a card through."

"What do we do then?"

"Well, the barrier will come up, an' then ya gan an' park up, an' take ya card an' paperwork in'a the customs hoos."

"Where's that?" I asked.

"Oh just get ya sel' inside man, an' get parked up, an' I'll come an' find ya an' sort ya oot."

Lewis kept his finger on the bottom button, just as the driver had told him, and a plastic card appeared, approximately the same size as a credit card.

"Hey up, we got a card, Bert! Cheers," Lewis said, as he took the card and the barrier went up. The Geordie ran back to his truck. I looked in the mirror as he went and saw that there was a bit of a queue behind us now.

I bet they're not best pleased with us.

We drove into the parking area and I couldn't believe my eyes.

It was massive! And there were trucks everywhere we looked, hundreds of them – no, thousands.

"Bloody 'ell Lewis, where are all this lot goin' to?"

"Or comin' from?"

A truck pulled up at the side of us – it was our Geordie friend. I collected the briefcase and the card, and Lewis picked up a new packet of shitanes. We both got out of the truck. The cold hit us immediately, after all, we had been kept warm by the truck's heater for so long. Also, my feet were feeling the cold and wet of the snow because I didn't have my boots on, as I was driving. All I had on my feet were what Douglas would describe as *'dancing shoes'*.

We hurried to catch up to our Geordie friend walking through the lines of trucks.

We introduced ourselves and he told us his name was Bob.

"Some motors in here, in't there, Bob?" I said.

"Waye aye, from all ova Europe, they gotta come inta this customs like, 'cause it's the main one for anywhere in Scandinavia, so it's full o' the buggas."

As we walked through, I noticed that some guys were fitting snow chains to their wheels.

"Don't like the look o' that Bob, 'cause we ain't got no chains."

"Well, me neither, but I don't give a monkey's chuff if I get stuck in the snow like - I'll just put the night heata on, a porno filum in the video, an' wait for the buggas ta dig me oot."

"We haven't got a night heater-"

"-or a video," added Lewis.

"Ya've naa night heata?" Bob asked in surprise. "Waye, y'al freeze ya fuckin' plum's off, man. It gets bastad cold up here, ya knaa."

"What, colder than Germany?" I asked.

"Waye aye man, an' you could end up having a run in with the pollass."

"How do you mean?"

"Well, they gan round all trucks that are parked up for the night, an' if they divn't hear a night heata runnin', or they notice you aven't got one fitted, they knock ya up an' make ya spend the night in an 'otel."

"Go and find a copper and tell him Bert, then perhaps we'll get a decent night's kip."

"Don't worry, we'll be in a hotel tonight kid, mark my words."

"Did ya bring that card with ya, like?" Bob asked.

"Yeah, I've got it here. What's the crack with this, then?"

"Ya need to 'and it to each customs person 'cause they

check ya movements wi' it. An' it's time-sensitive an' all, so don't be 'angin' aboot anywhere, like."

We'd been walking for at least five minutes and there was no sign of a building yet, just trucks.

"It's a fair size, this place, innit Bob? How big is it?"

"I divn't naa like," he said, "but it's aallas full, I've neva seen the bugga empty."

"Oh, d'you come here often then?" I asked, smiling.

"Aye, every week man," he said. It seemed he didn't catch on to my little pun.

"What've you got on?" Lewis asked.

"Hangin' garments, ya knaa, shirts an' that."

"Where you goin' with them?" I asked.

"Just ova the borda, a little toon called Abenra. I just drop the traila and hitch up to anotha bugga."

Lewis and I regaled him with the story of how we ended up in this part of the world. Bob told us that we were quite lucky to run into him, as British trucks were few and far between this far north. I remember when we got further north in Germany, Lewis had mentioned that he hadn't seen any British plates for a while.

We eventually arrived at the customs house. It was a huge brick building, with a set of glass swinging doors and, from what I could see, hardly any windows. Attached to the side of the building was a massive lean-to which had huge loading bays under it. Bob explained that this was where they would unload any suspicious trucks and check for drugs and such.

Up the steps and through the doors, we went down a short passageway that had doors to toilets and offices, and into a huge waiting room. The place was thick with smoke coming from the rows and rows of truckers sitting about, holding their relevant bits of paperwork and cigarettes. Some held A4-sized leather wallets, others had clipboards, some had the papers clutched in their hands, but none of them had a scruffy, old briefcase like ours. And, by the looks of them, if they had known what was inside it, a few of them might have tried to take it.

"There's some rum-looking buggers in here, Bob," I said.

"Aye, its them Swedes and Norwegians, they only need them 'ats wi' them 'orns on and they'd look like bloody Vikings."

"Right, what's the score in here, then?"

"Well, ya've t'gan ova there an' get a ticket..." he paused, thought for a moment, and said, "heea, just do what I do, man."

Bob took us over to the ticket dispenser, almost the same as the ones you get at the supermarkets, where you can queue at deli counters without losing your place. He told us that we had to watch the digital display board for our number to come up, and when it did, we had to look at another display board to find the corresponding window we had to go to when we went through the door marked *'told/zoll'*, or in English – customs.

As we were waiting for our number to appear, Lewis was telling Bob about the porn magazines on the counter in the petrol station.

"Waye aye, they divn't give a toss aboot a bit a'muff up hea man," he said, "if ya gan inta toon afta like, there's a fuckin' great sex shop on the main road, I get all me pornos from there."

"We'll have to have a look in there, eh Bert?" Lewis lifted his eyebrows as he looked at me.

Bloody unbelievable.

"Hey up, that's our number," I announced, "window twenty-three."

"Aye, that's reet like," confirmed Bob, "when ya get to window twen'y-three, give the guy behind the screen ya plastic card that ya got oot the machine by the barrier, he'll scan it and give it ya back. Then ya just carry on doon the corridor, through the next door an' inta Danish customs. When you're in the Danish side just gan to any window and give em ya card, ave ya got that lads?" said Bob smiling. There must have been a vacant look on both of our faces, because he continued in the same breath and said, "Divn't look so worried man, I'll not be far behind ya like."

We went through the door and up to our designated window. There was a very official-looking guy behind the glass in a smart, green, police-like uniform. I smiled at him and said hello, then passed our card to him. He put it into a machine next to him and looked at something on his computer screen. He then took the card out and gave it back to me.

"Papers," he said, looking at me.

"I haven't got any papers," I raised my palms to show that they were empty.

"Tell him we've got the *Daily Sport*," Lewis chuckled, hiding slightly behind the wall.

"Shuddup," I said out of the side of my mouth. "We're empty."

He looked at me for a brief moment. "No cargo?"

"Yes, no cargo."

"Ah, okay," he made a sweeping gesture with his arm, motioning us towards the exit door. I said goodbye, but the guy just busied himself while he waited for the next truck driver to appear at his window.

We went through the door to the Danish side of the building, and approached an empty window manned by a blonde girl with a very nice smile.

Much better than bloody Hitler next door.

She put the card in her machine, took a glance at the screen, and looked up at me. She said something in Danish, and I assumed she was asking what we were carrying.

"No cargo," I told her, but she looked at me as though I had grown two heads, so I repeated quickly, "er – we're empty, we're not loaded."

"Ah, you are English," she said with a lovely accent. "I need to have your truck and trailer numbers."

Oh, bloody hell. What's the trailer number now?

"HNE 436T," I recited, then I looked over at Lewis, "can you remember what the number on that trailer is?"

"Can I balls!"

Some bloody help you are.

"Hey, have a look in that briefcase, I'm sure you put the paperwork from Central Trailers in there."

I take it all back. Good ol' Lewis. He doesn't always come up with good ideas, but this time he has.

Sure enough, when I looked in the briefcase the paperwork was there, so I gave the girl the number. She wrote the details down and made me sign a piece of paper, I didn't know what it was for, for all I knew, I could have just signed my life away.

She gave me the card back and said goodbye.

As we made our way back to the truck, Lewis spotted a Bureau de Change.

"Hey Bert, Change de Boo-Row! Let's get some pastry money, eh?"

"Good idea, and it's called Danish money."

"Well, it's for buyin' pastries with, innit?" We ended up changing three hundred pounds of Dougal Arse's money into pastry money. "How much we got?" Lewis was looking at the bundle of money I had.

"Three thousand and summat krona."

"Fuck me! We're rich, kid!"

Leaving the building, we saw no sign of Bob, so we decided to go back to the truck. I was feeling rather pleased with myself. Here we were, in Denmark. We made it through all the necessary customs posts and we had finally arrived.

As I was walking down the passageway towards the glass doors, I noticed a guy coming in with a leather wallet under his arm and one of those Viking-like beards on his face.

When I passed him, I said in a loud, enquiring tone, *"Urrdy burddy gurddy?"*

Much to my pleasure, the guy turned around and tried to have a conversation with Lewis. I walked through the doors, laughing to myself.

"You bastard," Lewis laughed, once he caught up to me.

"What did he say?"

"How the fuck do I know? He was just *'hurddy gurddy'*-ing at me."

"He must've thought you were tryna talk to him."

"See, I told you that's all you have to say up here – *'urddy gurddy.'*"

We managed to find our way back to the truck and Lewis said we should celebrate with a smoke – I agreed, as long as we didn't have a shitane.

"I'll open these paddy cigs then."

"Which are them?"

"They're called Carrolls, you know Dina? *Dina Carroll?*"

"I know who she is, just give us a cig."

While we were having our smoke, Bob emerged out of the forest of trucks. We jumped down to talk to him, and he told us that we had to put our card into the box above the automatic barrier on the other side of the compound, and then we would be out and into Denmark. We thanked him and got back in the truck.

Jabba the Porn King

We were soon heading towards the town of Padborg. It had stopped snowing now, and it wasn't too slippery underfoot, but by God it was cold.

"How far off are we now, Bert?"

"Not far, it should just be on the other side of Padborg from what they told Dougal Arse when he rang them for directions."

Padborg was a nice, clean-looking place, with the houses and shops set back off the road. It all seemed rather quiet, given the time of day. In England, there would be people shuffling about on the pavements looking in shop windows, old men and women talking on street corners, and a few cars whizzing about. But there wasn't any of the expected day-to-day activity from the villagers in Padborg. It was strangely nice.

"Hey look Bert."

"What?"

"There," Lewis was pointing through the windscreen to a building down the street. The words *'SEX SHOP'* were proudly displayed in neon lights outside it. "Are we goin' in, or what?"

"Are we 'eck."

"Why not? It's only two o'clock, we've got loads o' time."

Why not? It might be a laugh.

We parked outside, as the roads were wide enough not to cause a problem for other motorists. As we were walking in the door, we heard two sharp blasts of a truck air horn, and looking around saw Bob powering past us.

"I bet he thinks we're a pair of perverts," said Lewis.

The shop was set out in a long triangular shape, with the door at the pointy end and the counter along the wide side opposite the door. Behind it sat the fattest guy I had ever seen. He must have been about thirty stone, with long, dark, greasy hair tied up in a ponytail and a goatee. I couldn't tell how tall he was because he was sitting down, but as we got closer I could see that he was slightly glistening with sweat, which I thought was quite an achievement, considering it was about minus ten degrees outside. I supposed that with the type of merchandise on sale, it went with the territory.

Whatever your sexual preference might be, I was sure that it would be catered for in this establishment. I, for one, had no idea what half of the contraptions were for. If there wasn't a sign outside saying 'sex shop', I would have thought we were in a car repair shop.

"What the fuck are them for?" Lewis asked, pointing to some car tyres on the floor with chains and handcuffs attached to them.

"Dunno, but I don't think they're for't snow," I laughed.

Lewis was in his element.

"Hey Bert, look at these videos," he shouted from the other side of the shop.

As I went around to him, I could feel the assistant's slitty eyes following my every move. I couldn't help thinking that if he didn't do anything about his weight, eventually his chubby cheeks would close his eyes permanently. Lewis was studying the racks of videos, presumably trying to decide which one to buy.

"There's every type of porno film here you could ever think of – look," he pointed to a video which had the word 'PAIN' written across the cover. There was a photograph of a man bent forwards, with his scrotum pierced and two very heavy-looking earrings hanging from the piercings. He also had a fist being shoved into his back passage. Well, at least the title's right. That sure looks like pain to me. "There must be some bloody weirdos 'round here, Bert."

"You're bloody right! So, are you gettin' this one, then?" I pointed at *PAIN*.

"Am I fuck," Lewis laughed, then he stopped as he realised what I said. "You cheeky sod, I'm not a bloody weirdo!"

"Hey up! What do you think's behind there?" I asked, motioning towards a curtained-off section of the shop. We turned to see Jabba looking over at us with his sweaty, puffed up face and half-closed beady eyes.

"What's in here?" Lewis called.

"Specialist," came the swift reply from Jabba.

"Fuckin' specialist?" Lewis turned back towards me. "Specialist? Fuck knows what's in there, Bert."

"Go and have a look if you want."

"No fuckin' way, I 'aint goin' in there. It'll be full of Jabba's mates, waitin' to rape me!"

We decided not to go into the specialist area, not even for a look. Something just didn't seem right about it, and given how explicit all of the merchandise on show outside was, I could only wonder what was behind closed curtains.

We went over to where the more 'normal' selection of videos were and Lewis picked a few up.

"How much is forty krona?"

"About four quid."

"Well, I'm gonna get twenty quid's worth, then."

"What are you gonna do with five porno films?"

"Watch 'em! What else you supposed to do with 'em?"

"Oh aye, where?"

"At home."

"Oh, I suppose you'll watch 'em with Maisie, will you? *It's one o'clock, is everybody comfortable? Welcome to* 'Watch Porno with Maisie!'" I said sarcastically.

"No, I'll wait while she goes to bed."

"While she goes to bed? She doesn't go to bed 'til about midnight."

"Alright, I'll sell 'em."

"Who to?"

"Tony P."

"Oh aye, he'll buy 'em."

Tony P was a mechanic who used to help us repair tractors and plant machinery at the farm. He was about five foot two, slightly rotund, and of Greek origin. The name Tony P originated from a friend of ours, and the 'P' stood for 'pervert', because all Tony ever seemed to talk about was sex, porn films, and the things he used to get up to on a beanbag at home with his wife.

"Hey, can you imagine bringin' Tony P in here?"

"Bloody 'ell, he'd be like a kid in a sweet shop!"

Lewis picked out five videos, all of which had dubious titles, including *The Italian (Blow) Job'*, *'A Fist Full of Fannies'*, and *'Dirty Harriet'*.

"I hope the films are better than the titles," I said.

"Aye, they are a bit suss, but Tony P won't mind."

"Five should last him a couple of days," I chuckled.

"I'll go and see if Jabba'll gimme any discount. Aren't you getting' anythin'?"

"Am I 'eck."

Lewis deposited his films on the counter and asked Jabba if he spoke English. "Of course," he replied. He then tried to get a discount for his bulk purchase, persuasively saying that nobody else would buy in such large quantities. Jabba told Lewis that had he been able to read Danish, he would have known that the minimum purchase was four videos anyway, to qualify for the *'Forty*

Kroner Each' price tag and, for his information, five videos was hardly a bulk order.

"Alright then," Lewis said defensively, "how do I know if they're any good?"

"Please," Jabba said, pointing towards a television screen fixed to the wall. He then put one of Lewis's videos into a VCR which was under the counter. As the television flickered to life and various couplings started to take place on screen, Jabba turned back to Lewis and said, with a wry smile on his face, "You may even masturbate if you like."

Lewis gave him a look that spoke volumes, while Jabba and I started laughing.

"Do you want to see them all?"

"No, that'll do," Lewis mumbled, obviously embarrassed.

I looked around as Jabba put Lewis's films in a plastic bag. Displayed in the shop were handcuffs, whips, dildos, edible knickers, and all sorts of other things, but just in front of the counter was a big wire basket full of what seemed to be rubber and plastic items.

"What's all this lot?" I asked Jabba.

"That is the discount barrel."

"Fuckin' discount barrel!" I laughed.

"Here," said Jabba, pulling something out of the barrel and putting it into Lewis's bag.

"What's that?" Lewis asked, pulling the item back out and scrutinising it. It was a rubber ring with what looked like a tiny little toy soldier on it.

"You pull it over your penis, to the bottom, and it stimulates your lady during sex."

"I'll never get that bugger on," said Lewis smugly, "unless you've got a shoe horn in your bargain bin, kid."

We collected Lewis's purchases and bade farewell to Jabba. Whilst Lewis had been checking the quality of the videos, I'd asked Jabba where Johansens was. The directions he gave me were easy enough to follow, and within forty minutes of driving we saw a flagpole displaying the logo and directing us towards the entrance.

Thank God for that, I can get rid of this bloody briefcase at last.

Not Another Bloody Night!

We turned into the entrance of Johansens, which was just off the main carriageway. The drive leading off it was wide and very long. I could tell that there had been quite a bit of traffic using it, because the snow was heavily compacted.

I couldn't see any buildings yet, just a small timber hut in a hammerhead off to the right, which I assumed must house the controls to the two fuel pumps that were situated either side of it. Further down the track, the sides had been raised to make loading platforms, which were constructed from huge timber posts set into the ground at about two-metre spacings, and long telegraph pole-like timbers stacked on top of one another to the rear, creating a barrier. They had been infilled at the back with soil to create an elevated platform. Christmas trees were stacked on them ready for loading onto trucks.

"I wonder if any of this lot are ours," I said as we passed by the stacks of trees to the left and right of us.

"There's bloody thousands!" Lewis said. "Shit job loadin' them though, with all that snow on top."

"Aye, it's bloody freezin' out there as it is, never mind havin' to mess about with that lot,"

Further down the track, we noticed some activity. As

we got closer, we could see two groups of four guys dressed in orange waterproofs. The groups were on either side of the track loading tilt-type trailers, just like the one we were pulling. They were parked up alongside the loading platforms, but the ones they were loading had been stripped back to the bones of the framework of the trailer for ease of loading. As we passed by the first group, they glanced over, and once a few of them had realised we were in a British truck, they stopped working and watched us go by.

I put my hand up in a wave, some of them acknowledged the gesture by waving back, but others just watched us go by.

"Did you see the faces on them, Lewis?"

"Aye, I bet they've never seen an old bastard like this up here before."

"I think it's just the fact we're British, they won't get many daft buggers like us comin' from England to pick their own trees up."

After about five minutes of steady driving over the snow, we arrived at a junction. It was a huge oak tree with timber palisade fencing around its base, creating a rustic roundabout. There were signs fastened to the fencing sending trucks to the left and cars to the right. We followed the arrowed directions into a huge yard, which had more tilt-type articulated trailers.

Some were loaded and some were waiting to load, most were just trailers, but there were one or two coupled up to German registered tractor units. Their drivers were inside the cabs, and they happened to notice we were in a right-hand drive truck. They looked on at us with amazement, just like the loading guys had done earlier.

"We're not bloody Martians," Lewis said at the window as we passed by the drivers.

"Well, Geordie Bob did say they don't see many Brits up this way."

We parked between a pair of loaded trailers, opposite a

two-story building. I could clearly make out the offices on the first floor through the windows that broke up the timber cladding, and by the look of the people coming to the window, they were interested in our arrival too.

"Right Lewis, let's get up in that office and see what the crack is."

"Should I bring the briefcase?" Lewis said sarcastically.

I ignored him and jumped out of the truck. We made our way up timber steps that led to the first floor offices.

The room was open plan, the office and reception areas were only broken up by a counter that had various bits of A4-size paper in neat little piles here and there, which I thought must be delivery documents.

There were about seven or eight people in the office, all at their desks; some typing, others on the phone. There was an even mix of men and women of varying ages.

Suddenly, a guy put his phone down and made his way over to us with a welcoming smile. He was about my age, six feet tall, quite slim, and wearing a pair of *John Lennon*-type glasses. He spoke in perfect English. "You must be the boys from England? My name is Dan, Dan Johansen."

"Hi Dan, I'm Jack and this is my brother, Lewis."

"Pleased to meet you," he said, shaking our hands. He gestured towards a small room behind us. "Would you like coffee?"

"Oh yes, please," replied Lewis.

We followed Dan into the little room and sat down at the table. Dan, being the perfect host, poured us a cup of coffee each out of a glass pot that was kept warm on an electric hob. He also produced a box that was about the same size as a small suitcase. He put the box on the table in front of us and opened the lid to reveal that it was full of the infamous Danish pastries that we had always heard about.

I hope Lewis leaves them a few.

I laughed to myself. I could almost visualise us eating nothing but Danish pastries for the rest of the trip.

"Please help yourselves to a pastry," Dan offered.

A woman came in and said something to Dan in Danish, politely acknowledging Lewis and I.

"Enjoy your coffee, I will return in a moment," said Dan as he stood up and followed the woman out of the room.

"*A* pastry?" said Lewis, incredulously. "I'm fuckin' 'ank – I'll be havin' more than one!"

"You're right there, kid. They won't miss a few, get them down you. We might not get 'owt to eat for a bit, 'cause it'll take a while to load up."

We started to stuff various pastries into our mouths. I bet we looked like a right pair of scruffy buggers, we hadn't shaved or bathed since Saturday night, and it was now Tuesday afternoon.

Dan came back into the room and asked us if everything was okay. Struggling to swallow our mouthful of pastry, we said it was fine, and I asked him when we could get loaded. Dan explained that we wouldn't be loading the trees out of the yard, but at three farms further into Denmark on the island of Fyn, which he pronounced Foon, about three hours away. He said that because of the price Douglas had negotiated for the trees, it wasn't cost effective for Dan to transport them to his yard, which was why we had to travel deeper into Denmark to get them. He was very apologetic, but it wasn't really his fault, so we resigned ourselves to the fact that we would be spending another night in the cab with the company of that bloody briefcase.

Another guy entered the room then. He was roughly six feet six tall, about eighteen stone, and all rugged up against the cold. He walked straight over to the table, and without even looking at us he flipped open the lid of the box of pastries and started eating them.

"This is my brother, Bo," said Dan.

"Alreet," we both said. Bo grunted and looked up slightly. Dan asked Bo to give us directions to the loading

133

places on Fyn, where we had to pick up the trees.

Bo wasn't as ignorant as I had suspected, he just wasn't as confident as his brother. After half an hour of looking at maps and drawing map sketches, we were armed with addresses and directions of, hopefully, our final destinations.

Dan then asked if we wanted to ring the UK, so I thought I better phone the farm with an update.

Sally, Douglas's sister, answered.

"Hello?"

"Hello," Sally's voice came through the receiver, "oh, Bertie!" she said, realising who it was. "Where are you? Are you in Denmark yet? What are the trees like? Are you loaded?"

"Bloody 'ell, give us chance. Er – yes, dunno, and no. Does that answer your questions?"

"Do you want to speak to Douglas?"

"No," I explained that there was no point speaking to him yet, as we had nothing to report about the trees because we were going elsewhere to load. I said we would phone again when we got loaded up.

We gave our thanks to Dan and Bo for letting us use the phone and said our goodbyes. It was getting dark rather quickly now, so we wasted no time in getting back into the truck and out of the yard.

"We're gonna be kippin' in here again tonight, aren't we?" asked Lewis.

"Looks like it."

"I'm not lookin' forward to it, it's gonna be bloody cold."

"I know. Sorry, kid, but there's nowt I can do about it."

"I know, let's just see if we can find a decent services or summat near to where we're headin'."

"I'll try kid. Anyway, stop moanin' and let's have a Dina."

"Aye, alright. I think I'll have a can of beer as well, seein' as we aren't loadin' or owt," said Lewis, looking considerably cheered up.

"Aye, give me one as well," I joked.

Fully Allowed

"Hey! What do you reckon was behind them curtains at Jabba's?"

"I dunno, but it must've been some fucked up stuff."

"I know, it doesn't bear thinkin' about, does it?"

"To be honest, it was probably that fat bugger's dinner, and he didn't want anybody pinchin' it!" laughed Lewis.

After a couple of hours driving, we pulled in at a service station just outside the city of Odense. The truck parking area was strangely deserted, apart from a few cars parked here and there. It seemed odd, because by this time in Germany, the truck parks were always full.

"I don't like the look of this, Lewis."

"Look of what?"

"There's no bloody trucks."

"So?"

"Well, trucks might not be allowed to park in here overnight."

"Well, there's only one way to find out," Lewis grabbed the briefcase and opened the door, "we'll have to go in."

We walked over to the service building. It looked more like the services at home, unlike the restaurant-type ones we had gotten used to in Germany. This was more like a

Little Chef. Just through the entrance door were the toilets, so I went to use them and Lewis went to the cafeteria section.

When I had finished I entered the cafeteria in search of Lewis. I spotted him talking to a waiter, who left when I got to the table.

"You haven't ordered what you think is bloody bangers and mash again, have you?"

"Have I 'eck. No, I just asked him if it was alright to park up for the night with the truck."

"Well, what did he say?"

"I know you're not gonna believe me, but he sounded like Arnie!" Lewis laughed.

"Bollocks! It's you, you think they all talk like Arnie!"

"Listen to him when he comes back, then."

The waiter returned carrying two bottles of Tuborg lager.

"I see you got your priorities right," I said, eyeing the beer.

"Is it okay to park overnight with the truck?" Lewis asked the waiter.

"Yes, it is fully allowed," he said in a stern, monotone voice.

I had to admit, he did sound just like Arnie. We started talking to him, and found out that he was a student, and he was quite excited about having us in his cafeteria because he could practise his English. Apparently, he didn't get to see many English people, as they only visited Copenhagen.

When he walked away, Lewis started laughing, "See – fuckin' Arnie!"

After a few more Tuborgs and a nice dinner of meatball and chips, we decided to head back to the truck. We waved goodbye to the waiter and his young, blonde female colleague.

Lewis shouted over to them, "Will you send her 'round to the truck in about ten minutes, so I can throw me bones on her?"

"Fully allowed," I said in my best Arnie voice.

We swung open the double doors, which lead us out into the dark, Denmark night. As we emerged from the warmth of the cafeteria, our feet made a crisp, crackling noise on the snow beneath our feet. I could feel the frost in the air biting on my face, and our breath came out in wisps.

"Bloody 'ell, its cold! When we get in, get that stove fired up."

Once we were settled in the truck, Lewis plugged the holes where the draughts had been coming in and put a pair of overalls on, in anticipation of the cold night ahead.

"What we on kid, shitanes or Dina's?"

"Oh, I think we'll have Dina's," Lewis said, digging a packet of Carrolls cigarettes out of our duty-free stash under the bunk. "Here you are, get that cracked too," he passed over a bottle of red wine.

"Who would've thought this time last week that we'd be sat in this peaty old wagon in the middle of Denmark, on a near deserted service station, freezin' our bollocks off, suppin' red wine, and smokin' Irish cigs?"

"Aye, you sure know how to show a girl a good time," laughed Lewis.

As I tipped the last of the wine out in our glasses – well, mugs – I said to Lewis, "Fuck 'em, shall we crack another?"

"Fully allowed!"

We then had a debate about what people meant when they said 'fuck 'em'. Fuck who, we wondered? The level of conversation was hardly academic, but we had a laugh and put our little bit of the world to rights, sitting in an eight-by-six foot box mounted on top of an engine.

"We'll get goin' a bit handy in the mornin' Lew, as soon as it gets light."

"Well, I'll be up. I always am in this thing."

"We'll get loaded up and leave the truck at one of the farms we're loadin' at, find a hotel, and get a good meal

Fully Allowed

down us, maybe a little session on the drink."

"Oh aye, a proper bed. I think I'll just get in it when we get there, and have all my food sent to the room."

"Aye, well, so long as you don't sign the sheets like you did on the ferry!" I laughed.

"You're never gonna let me forget about that one, are you?"

"You're bloody right I'm not!"

"You better not tell anyone back home."

"I won't, but it might be handy when you get somethin' on me, so we'll be able to do a deal."

"Don't worry, I'll find summat."

"I tell you what, I could do with a gypsies, but I don't fancy goin' out there and lettin' the cold in."

"Well, don't piss on me. Here, fill one of these up," Lewis passed me an empty beer can, "that's what I've been doin' all the other nights when you were kippin', 'cause I didn't like goin' out gettin' cold after takin' so long to get warm."

"Better make sure we don't pick the wrong ones up then, eh, you scruffy sod," I passed him the can I had just relieved myself in. "Thanks."

"Fuckin' 'ell, it's nearly full. Good job we aren't suppin' them half-cans. Otherwise you'd have had to snap it off mid-piss!" Lewis wound the window down enough to get the can through and tipped the contents outside.

"I hope there's nobody out there watchin'."

"Well, I'm not havin' cans o' piss all over the cab."

"They would've been handy the other night, if them Turks had tried to do 'owt to you."

"I tell you what, after that Tuborg stuff we supped in there," he gestured towards the services, "we should save a couple of cans for the diesel tank – it's bloody strong stuff, that."

"Aye, we've had some good pop on this trip, but I think we've deserved it, don't you?"

"We have, and I think we deserve one last shitane, then

139

we'll turn in." He passed me a cigarette and lighter.

A few minutes after we had settled down for the night, Lewis said, "Jack."

"What?"

"It's about your fartin'."

"What d'you mean? I haven't farted all night," I said defensively.

"I know - that's the trouble, I wish you would. It might make it a bit bloody warmer in here."

"Stop whingin', if you're that cold, why don't you have a wank?"

"I just might," he chuckled.

"You better not, if anyone's outside, they'll think we're the *Elton John* brothers."

Bo's Rubbish Directions

The next morning was as cold as I had ever experienced – ice had actually formed on the inside of the window. I didn't fancy getting out from under the covers, so I could imagine how Lewis felt. The other mornings waking in the truck, I could feel the cold on my face, but this morning I could feel it in my bones.

It was dark and I needed some inspiration to motivate me into life.

"C'mon Lewis kid," I roused, gesturing for him to make a move and get himself up and at 'em.

His reply was swift, "Fuck off, it's the most comfortable I've been all bloody night."

"I know, it's normally the case."

I looked down on Lewis. I couldn't help feeling sorry for him. I knew how uncomfortable it had been for me, and I had a bed. Well, if you could call it a bed.

In my best rallying voice I said, "C'mon Lewis, let's get sorted in here. Then we'll go up to your mate's, get a bit of a wash, a brew and some food, and you'll feel a lot better." He just lay there, saying nothing. "Listen kid, I promise you, whatever happens today, we're stoppin' in a hotel tonight."

"Promise?" he mumbled, turning his head to look at me.

"Promise. But we can't get to a hotel if you won't get outta bloody bed, you idle sod."

"Oh, alright. Stop whingin'. I'm gettin' up."

"The sooner we get on the road and get these bloody trees loaded, the sooner we can get some digs."

Lewis dragged himself up off the engine cowling to sit on the seat. I noticed that he had two pairs of overalls on, not just the one pair he had put on the night before.

"Them mine?"

"What?"

"Overalls."

"Yeah, sorry. I woke up fuckin' freezin' durin' the night, so I found yours and put them on. S'alright, innit?"

"Yeah, no prob. I wondered what you were doin' actually, I felt the cab shakin' 'cause you were movin' about. I thought you were havin' a wank, so I didn't say anythin'."

"Listen, I was that cold last night that if I'd had a wank I'd probably have snapped it off!" he laughed.

"Hey, that's the spirit, our kid. C'mon, let's go in and get some breakfast, see if that little blonde's workin' this mornin'. She'll warm you up." I opened the curtains to see a fair few trucks and cars dotted about. "It's a bit busier than last night out there, our kid."

We jumped down out of the truck – me, Lewis, and our friend, the bloody briefcase. It was beginning to feel like one of those mates that nobody likes, but for some reason is always there when you go out. We crunched our way over the snow on the service area car park and into the welcome warmth of the cafeteria. It was still dark outside, but I could just make out the light peeping over the horizon, looking for us.

Lewis and I made a beeline straight for the toilets, burst into a cubicle each and, as they say, the rest is history. Well, for me it was. All I could hear from the next cubicle was Lewis struggling to take off all his layers.

While I was washing my hands, Lewis emerged from his cubicle, remarking on the close call he had just had, and that now he was too warm.

"Always bloody whingin'," I laughed, "c'mon."

I opened the door of the toilets and stepped out into the passageway leading to the cafeteria.

"Hold on Bert, I'm gonna have to take these overalls off – I'm fuckin' boilin'!"

"Aye, alright. I'll go and get some snap ordered, sausage butties and a Tuborg do you?" I opened the door to the cafeteria smiling.

"Yeah, whatever," called Lewis sarcastically, hopping about on one leg as he was trying to shed his overalls.

The cafeteria was quite busy. Not full, but busy enough for me to walk in without feeling as if everyone was looking at me. I found a table and ordered sausages, bread, and a pot of coffee. I wouldn't drink coffee normally, but we found the continental type to be very nice indeed. Maisie wouldn't have liked it though.

'Can't beat Nescafe!' she'd say.

Oh yes you can, Mam.

Lewis made his way over to me and sat down, looking at me expectantly.

"What've you ordered, kid?"

"Sausages, bread, and a big pot of coffee."

"Ooh, just nice."

We ate our breakfast like we hadn't eaten for a week. It must have been the cold of the night which made us so hungry. The staff were different to the guys who had been on the night before, and like their colleagues from the previous evening, they were very interested in talking to us. They were a nice bunch of people, but unfortunately they couldn't afford us the same attention, as the cafeteria was far busier than it had been the previous evening.

We paid for our breakfast, and said goodbye while they wished us good luck. Through the double doors and out onto the car park, we had a new found energy, crunching our way back into Big Edith. All the truck checks were done, the tachograph chart in, and there was only one thing left to do.

Vroom!

"Seems this old bastard can stand the cold better than us, Lew!"

Once we pulled onto the motorway network, it was obvious that the roads were not as busy as the ones in Germany had been. I supposed that the only place this road was ultimately going was the Danish capital of Copenhagen.

We followed Bo's directions to the letter, and pulled off the motorway at the junction he had given. We were heading south on the country lanes towards our destination, Svendborg. On arrival, we had instructions to find a phone box and call Johansens' agent to arrange for him to meet us and take us to the locations of the trees.

As we progressed further into Fyn, the roads that Bo had mapped out for us to follow started to get quite narrow, but we weren't too alarmed. I thought that they were very much like the country lanes in England. We passed a bunch of orange, boiler-suited council workers, who took a moment out from staring down their hole to watch us pass. Orange must have been the chosen colour of workwear in Denmark.

"I tell you what," Lewis said, "it's like bein' a bloody film star in this truck. They all stare at you, don't they?"

"Aye," We rounded a corner. Then I realised why they had been staring at us. Because they knew something we didn't. In front of us was a railway bridge unlike any we had seen before. We were used to Mr Brunel's arched brick type, but this one was a long, steel tube set on concrete columns. It must have done the job just the same, but it looked very modern, very smart, and very low. To the underside of the bridge, the clearance was three metres – and our overall truck height was four point two.

"Fuckin' Bo! The pastry-chewin' bastard!"

"He probably sent us this way on purpose," Lewis laughed, "for eatin' some of his pastries."

A couple of cars had built up behind us now, but as we were on a bend it was difficult for them to negotiate getting around the truck.

"You're gonna have to get out Lew, and direct the traffic around us."

We both ended up getting out of the truck. Luckily for us though, it wasn't a very busy road, and we soon had the cars moving around us. I ran up the road, because I was sure that I had seen a side road that maybe I could reverse into. Well, I hoped that I had seen one. I didn't fancy reversing all the way to where those council guys were, which must have been at least a mile back.

With a huge surge of relief, I found the side road. I got back to Lewis and told him what I intended to do. I started the truck and, with Lewis watching me and diverting the traffic, manoeuvred into the side road without a hitch. It was lucky that the traffic was very light, and any drivers that we did encounter went by with an understanding nod or wave, unlike in England, where we would have received the usual barrage of abuse and horn-blowing.

Lewis jumped back into the truck and we set off back the way we had come, wondering which way we should go next.

"Here, pull over," Lewis instructed, "these buggers'll know how to get where we wanna go." I pulled up next to the group of council guys and their van. Lewis got out and said, "Alright," as he approached them. They looked at him as though he had just stepped out of a spaceship. I got out as well, to make sense of any information that Lewis would manage to get out of them.

It was obvious that none of the guys could speak English and, as we didn't understand any Danish, it was quite an achievement that after about ten minutes of hand gestures, we had a good idea of where to go next to reach our destination.

As we pulled away they all piled into their van and set off in the opposite direction. Lewis said that they were probably going back to the council yard to tell their mates about the two scruffy Englanders they had just sent off to Poland.

The directions the council guys gave us got us back onto the motorway network, around the outskirts of Fyn, and ultimately into Svendborg. We trundled through the village looking for a public phone box to ring Johansens' agent. When we eventually found one it was made of glass, but us two idiots were looking for the usual, post-office red, like we would find at home. I was relieved when I found out that the procedure for ringing someone was the same as it was at home, and fished in my pocket for some coins.

Good job we changed some money.

The person at the end of the phone answered immediately. He introduced himself as Peter, told us to stay where we were, and he would find us in about ten minutes.

The Trolls

The Danes had a brusque, curt manner of speaking, which I was slowly getting used to, and Peter was no different. It wasn't as if they weren't friendly or polite, but that their delivery of the English words were somehow without emotion. Lewis and I lovingly referred to this as the 'Arnie Effect'.

It was a beautiful day. Clear blue skies, with just a breath of icy eastern wind. Apart from the odd bird chirping – probably telling her mate to get out of bed and find some worms for breakfast – there was not a sound in the air. The village, with its pointy roofed houses, looked like a picture from the front of a Christmas card. It was all so clean and fairy tale-like. It gave me a comforting feeling.

Lewis was pawing through his magazine, showing me a few pictures and laughing. He said that he wished he could read German, because then at least he could read the articles.

Yeah, whatever Lewis!

With the engine switched off, Big Edith wasn't generating any heat, and I could feel the cold wrapping around my legs. I contemplated starting her up again, and glanced over at Lewis. He was happy enough for the minute, deep in his magazine. I don't think he even noticed it was getting cold.

I looked around the cab, which was in a bit of a state. Different types of cigarette packets were strewn about; some nearly empty, some half empty, others with a few missing.

Plenty of them bloody shitanes left though, we could do with smokin' them buggers and getting rid. It could do with a good tidy up in here too - get Maisie in!

I chuckled to myself, and Lewis looked over.

"What you laughin' at?"

"Nothin', just that it's a fuckin' dump in here."

"Hey! It's our dump though Bert," he said, looking around the cab.

"Good job, 'cause no one else would want it," I laughed. "Here, do you want a shitane?" I passed them over to him.

"Fuck that, give us a Dina, you need to be pissed to smoke them Shitanes!"

We finished our Dinas and talked about the possibility of staying in a hotel that night. I for one couldn't do another night in here, and I had a 'bed'. Lewis must have been desperate for a good night's sleep. As we were talking, I looked in the mirror and noticed a Land Rover approaching us from behind. It drove past and stopped in front of the truck.

"Hey up, I think we're on here," I said.

Out jumped a guy who came over to Lewis' side of the truck and identified himself as Peter. He told us, in perfect English of course, which direction we were going to follow him.

Lewis promptly stopped him and explained that he wasn't the driver. Peter looked to my side of the cab and shook his head, smiling. He looked to be around thirty-something, quite tall, slim, and with a tightly trimmed full beard.

We both got out of the truck and introduced ourselves

properly, requesting that we get loaded as soon as possible. I also asked if he could point us in the direction of a good hotel, which made Lewis beam.

Formalities over, we jumped back in the truck and followed Peter in his Land Rover. We left the village and started travelling through the boring Danish countryside. It bore all the hallmarks of Shropshire for me, with sandy, silty soil level to undulating fields, broken up with huge plots of Christmas trees.

As I was admiring the scenery, Peter turned left off the main road onto a narrow lane. We followed him for about a mile, to where a patch of Norway Spruce trees lay on an elevated grass bank at the side of the road.

Standing in a half-circle around the pile of freshly chopped trees were a group of five really tall, heavily built guys, dressed in boiler suits and baseball caps. They reminded me of a bunch of red-neck hillbillies. Or trolls. Knuckle-dragging trolls, protecting their pile of trees. As we approached, they lifted their heads in turn to look towards our advancing truck.

We pulled up alongside the pile of trees and emerged from Big Edith, feeling the crisp winter air on our faces and in our lungs. "Bloody 'ell, it's colder than I thought," I said, rubbing my hands together.

Approaching the guys, Peter was introducing us to the trolls in Danish, who smiled and shook our hands. Theirs were huge and rough, it was like shaking hands with five rusty coal shovels, making me feel like a schoolboy.

God, I used to think I was well hard[21] before I met these guys.

Peter spoke to the lead troll who grunted orders to his comrades. On his command, they each picked up a Christmas tree by the butt end and offered them to us, like a child would present you with a used lollipop stick.

"Whoa! Hold on a minute," I said firmly.

The trolls still holding out the trees looked to each

---

[21] Tough

other and then to Peter for guidance. Peter glanced over at me with a confused expression.

"I need to open up the trailer first," I explained, "just give us five minutes."

Peter informed the lead troll of our intentions who then conveyed the message to the others. They all nodded to him, turning to look back in our direction, still holding the trees in front of them like some sort of peace offering. The guys must have been at least seven feet tall, and very powerful-looking. I certainly wouldn't want any trouble with them.

"Fuck me," whispered Lewis, as we readied the trailer. "They're big nobheads, aren't they?"

"You're not wrong there our kid, don't you go upsettin' them or comin' out with any of that Arnie shit," I said smiling, turning my head slightly to look at the trolls, who all smiled back in eerie silence.

"Don't you worry about that," said Lewis, jumping into the trailer. "Hey," he added smiling, "it's like that film, *The Hills Have Eyes*. Mind you don't get eaten, our kid!"

"Shut up you idiot," I said, turning back to face our hosts. "Ok, we're ready," I announced. The trolls all looked at the lead guy, who then looked at Peter who gave them permission to begin loading.

The trolls formed a human chain and, using only one hand, passed the trees to each other like a well-trained relay team. The needles on the trees where sharp, sticking into our skin, and we had gloves on, but this didn't seem to bother the gloveless trolls as they happily passed the trees along. I noticed that the quality of the trees was poor, and reluctantly had to bring proceedings to a swift stop.

I explained to Peter that the quality wasn't very good and I only wanted to load the better ones. He replied that he was only following instructions from Johansens, and these were the trees that we had to load, so I asked if he would call Johansens on his mobile. While Peter was on the phone, I tried to explain to the lead troll what the problem was. He looked down on me silently, smiling and nodding his head. He then said something to his colleagues, who all laughed in unison whilst looking me up and down. Just as I was wondering if we were going to get away with our bodies still intact, Lewis shouted, "Urddy Gurrdy!" from deep within the bowels of the trailer. The trolls looked over at the truck.

Fuckin' idiot.

I tried not to laugh.

In the nick of time, Peter returned from his phone call and confirmed that we could cherry-pick the better trees. He gave fresh orders to the guys, who grunted and moved aside to allow me through to grade the trees. I walked furtively passed them, ever conscious of their towering stature.

Gee, I used to think that I was tall at six foot two, but these guys are makin' me feel like a fuckin' hobbit!

I rummaged through the pile of trees, grading them as I went, placing the good ones to the left, and the others to the right. With a grunt and a puff, I offered the trees up with both hands, and my new work colleagues looked down on me, taking them one handed with a breathless smile. It didn't take very long, with our well-oiled machine of giants, to load our preferred trees.

When the loading was finished, we tied up the trailer and jumped back into Big Edith. We gave the trolls a wave as we pulled away. They all smiled and waved back with their big leathery hands. Taking time out from reloading the unwanted trees onto a farm trailer that they had with them, I couldn't help wondering whether they had pulled the trailer with a tractor or carried it themselves.

"Now they were Arnies," Lewis said, lighting a cigarette and passing it over.

"You're bloody right," I laughed.

Peter then took us to a little farm about an hour away

from the last loading spot. He told me to park on the road and he would take me up in the Land Rover to where the trees were, because it wouldn't be easy to get a truck in and should we not like them it would have wasted time to try. I agreed and jumped in with him, Lewis said he would stay with the truck.

When I got there, I saw that the trees were excellent, so we loaded our quota of Scotch Pine trees and the rest of the Norway order. All we had to do now was get to the final loading place for a thousand Nordmann Firs. These were the trees we had originally come for, the others we had got had just been to make the load up and make transport costs cheaper. We had only loaded a few hundred trees so far, so we had plenty to do, but the day was disappearing fast. By the time we got there and readied the trailer for loading, it was starting to go dark.

We started to load the trees, and it was obvious that some of them weren't very good, so I stopped the loading to have a word with Peter about the quality. He agreed with the farmer to pre-select the trees before they went onto the truck.

After we had loaded about two hundred and fifty trees, I stopped proceedings again, explaining that I wasn't happy about loading in the dark, as we couldn't really see what we were getting. I asked, if they had no objections, could we leave the truck here and continue in the morning. Like the gentlemen they were, everybody agreed to be back in the morning to start loading again at nine o'clock.

Peter loaded us and our things, including that dreaded briefcase, into his Land Rover, and took us to a hotel in a village some twenty minutes away.

"I hope we can get in," I wondered aloud.

"No problem," Peter said, "when you asked me where to stay this morning, I phoned the office and they booked you in."

"Brilliant!" Lewis was positively giddy, beaming from ear to ear.

We had been so busy during the day that although it was only five o'clock in the evening, it felt much later. Peter dropped us off outside the hotel, but popped in to make sure that everything was okay with the booking.

He came out with his thumbs up and said, "You will have a good night in there – good food and good drink."

"Lookin' forward to it," Lewis said, "any good women?"

"I don't know, but if there are, I'm sure you boys will find them," he replied, smiling.

We said our goodbyes to Peter and he arranged to pick us up at half past eight in the morning.

"Right," I picked my bag and briefcase up and led the way into the hotel, "we'll check in, have a swift 'un, and get washed and changed for dinner."

"You're on," replied Lewis.

Gunpowder, Cockneys, and Beer

The hotel was like a big house, akin to a B&B at home. We checked ourselves in and made our way around to the small bar. There were a couple of guys already there drinking beer. As we approached, they gave us a quick glance and then looked away before they made eye contact. I wasn't surprised. We must have looked like a rather desperate pair by now.

We stood at the bar waiting to be served, muttering amongst ourselves, because there wasn't a lot of noise in the place. In fact, it was quite dead, but considering the time of day, I didn't think anything of it.

Eventually, the young girl who had checked us in came to serve our drinks. It seemed like she had a few jobs to do, apart from working on reception. She was blonde, slim, and very pretty, with a lovely smile.

I wouldn't mind findin' her a job.

"Two Tuborgs, please," I asked her.

"Tuborg?" She had a lovely accent.

"Yes, please," I was trying to act cool.

"Hey up, she's off." said Lewis.

"What y'on about?"

"You, flirtin' with her."

"Hey, I'm just bein' polite!"

"Polite, my arse! I've known you too long, our kid. I know when you're tryna pull."

"Nowt wrong with tryin'."

"Oh, I agree, but you don't stand a chance, kid."

"How do you make that out?"

"Your friend is right," came a voice from over my shoulder.

I turned around and the two guys who were at the bar as we came in were looking at us in anticipation of a response. As we hadn't heard them clearly, we said "Alright," and turned back to roll our eyes at each other.

"Are you English?" asked the guy behind us in a familiar accent.

That's all we need, a fuckin' cockney.

"Yeah," I replied, turning to face the two guys with half a smile.

"Hi," he held his hand out for me to shake, "I'm Harry and this is Olaf." We shook hands and said our hellos.

The two guys were from Norway and had a pyrotechnic company. They were here to make a television programme for Danish TV, but they explained that they had trouble getting through Danish customs with the gunpowder and detonators. It was understandable of course, even though they had all the necessary paperwork. They said that the customs guys wouldn't let them through with everything, so they had to make a decision on whether to take the detonators or the gunpowder. They decided on the detonators, because they assumed that they could pick up gunpowder easier than detonators.

"Oh aye, you'll get that in Tesco," laughed Lewis.

"Tesco?" Olaf said, looking puzzled.

"British sense of humour, Olaf," Harry explained.

They told us that they were relying on this job to put them on the road to success, as they had only worked on small theatre productions in Norway. This was their big break, working for a TV company, but as they only had half of their equipment, they were worried that they might be fired before they had even started.

Harry told us that he had lived in Norway for about six years. He had originally moved out there with a Norwegian girl he had met in London while she was at University, but they split up after a couple of years. He said he had a hard time getting citizenship, but now that he had it, he wouldn't return back to England. Not that Norway was wholly better, he told us, just different.

After a couple more drinks, we decided it was time to go and survey the rooms and have a good, long overdue wash. We said goodbye to the lads and told them that we might see them later at dinner.

The rooms weren't bad at all, with en suite, phone, television, and a nice big double bed that I flopped down on. I closed my eyes, going over the trip so far in my mind, and then the phone rang.

He never misses a chance. Well, bollocks to him! I'll let it ring.

But the phone didn't stop, so I got up, picked the phone up and said, "Fuck off, Arnie."

"I'm sorry," came the reply, the voice of which I recognised as the girl from reception.

"Oh, hello," I muttered, embarrassed.

"Have you left a bag in the bar, sir?"

My heart dropped as I realised it was that bloody briefcase.

"Shit, yeah. I mean, yes, thank you. I'll come right down and get it."

"Thank you," she said, rather abruptly, putting the phone down.

Have I upset her? Maybe it was my swearin'?

It was a strange thing, vanity. I was nearly as worried about upsetting her as I was of losing the briefcase. I went downstairs to look for it.

There it was, leaning against the now empty bar, where I had so casually left it. The two guys we had been talking to were gone, but they could quite easily have taken it.

When I stood up, the receptionist was behind the bar.

"Okay?" she asked with a smile.

Oh good, she hasn't fallen out with me.

"Okay," I reassured her, "and thank you very much."

When I turned to go back up to the room, a terrible thought hit me.

Is the money still there, or have them two buggers nicked it?

But they'd need to have a key.

Well, they might've had one, or been able to pick a lock, especially that cockney.

I started to climb the stairs.

I'm sure it feels lighter than before. There'll be nowt in it - the money's gone!

I fumbled with the key in the lock, pushed open the door to my room, and threw the briefcase on my bed.

The locks look okay, thought the optimistic side of my brain.

But then, those thieves are good, thought the pessimistic side. I fished the key out of my pocket and opened it.

Just get the fuckin' thing open, Jack.

I threw back the lid and there it was, wrapped up in its little cotton Barclays bank bag.

Phew!

Or is it?

It could just be newspapers.

I tipped out the contents of the bag to satisfy all corners of my mind and counted the money. Thankfully, it was all there and it made me realise that there were still plenty of honest people in the world. It just didn't seem so sometimes.

The phone started to ring again, well, if you could call it a ring. It was more like the horn of a toy car.

"Hello?" I said, ever so politely.

"Asshole," came the reply. The bugger had got me again. I thought it might have been the girl from reception.

"Where've you been kid? I've rung twice," asked Lewis.

"I'll tell you when we have our tea. I'm havin' a shower

and that now, so I'll ring you in about twenty minutes."

"Don't bother," replied Lewis, "I've had a bath and a shave, so I'm nearly ready. I'll see you down in the bar after."

"Okay, but don't be getting drunk."

"I won't, I'll just concentrate on chattin' your bird up."

"Hey, leave her alone!"

"First come, first served," Lewis laughed, putting the phone down.

God Bless You, Vera

After I got ready, I thought it best to ring Douglas and tell him what was happening.

I sat on the edge of the bed waiting for the phone to connect, thinking about how he'd start whinging about the trees if I tell him the quality wasn't very good.

If he wasn't such a tight bastard, then we wouldn't have had to argue with the loaders and-

"Hello, Meadow Heights," Sally answered the phone.

"Hi Sally, it's Jack. Is Doug –"

"Jack," she interrupted, "you must ring your Mum."

Sally explained that our Auntie Vera, Mam's only sibling, had died sometime the previous week, and that the funeral was the day after tomorrow. Mam didn't know her sister had died. She didn't even know that Vera had been admitted to hospital. It was only when Sharon, Vera's daughter, asked her dad where Auntie Maisie would be staying for the funeral that he realised he hadn't told our Mam. Uncle Stan suffered badly from Parkinson's disease, and he was devastated by the loss of his wife, so it was understandable that he wasn't thinking straight. The worst of it was that Mam wouldn't be able to go down to Cornwall for the funeral, as she wouldn't be able to get there in time.

I gave Sally my thanks and a brief run-down of what was happening. She told me not to worry about anything and to ring home.

I went down to the bar and saw Lewis sat by himself, staring into space.

"Have you got me one?"

"No, I didn't know how long you were gonna be."

As he finished talking, the receptionist/barmaid appeared from the back of the bar, smiling in my direction.

Well, there you go, we must look like human beings again.

"Yes?" The girl asked, in that abrupt manner she did on the phone earlier.

She probably doesn't mean anythin' by it, it's just the way these people are.

"Two Tuborgs please," I said with a smile.

When she walked away to get them, Lewis said, "Ooh, she must like you – when I came down, she didn't come out for ages!"

She came back, and I asked her what time the restaurant opened. She said eight o'clock, and when I enquired if she worked in there as well, she assured us she did.

"Do you cook, as well?" I asked, flirting openly.

"No, just the tables. I will tell you when the restaurant is ready. Enjoy your drinks," she replied, smiling.

"Thank you, and we will."

"Well? D'you think you'll pull her, kid?"

"I don't know, but we'll have to ring Maisie after."

"What for?"

I told Lewis about Vera - we called her Viv - and how she had died.

"That's typical of Stan," said Lewis, "he just doesn't want any of us lot down there," Vera had lived in Truro in Cornwall. "The old bastard, he never liked me."

"Well, I'm not surprised, with some of the stuff you and our Cliff used to get up to when you went to stay."

"I dunno what you mean."

"For a start, you used to call him Uncle Spam instead of Uncle Stan, pretendin' you couldn't pronounce his name properly. That used to wind him up. And then you and Cliff used to spend most of the time takin' the piss out've his ears."

"Oh aye, he's got some lugs[22] on him, Uncle Spam."

Lewis recounted the time he and Cliff had been stopping with Stan and Vera for a week long holiday.

Stan and Vera went to bed earlier than Lew and Cliff were used to, especially when they were on holiday. It was only about ten o'clock in the evening. It wasn't going to bed early that was the problem, it was the fact they were hungry. Well, Lewis was peckish and Cliff was hungry, that was the trouble. I wouldn't say that our Cliff was fat, but he was a big lad, and his figure took some looking after.

So they decided to sneak to the kitchen and see if there was anything to eat. On a scale of one to ten, the chances of them sneaking anywhere was – at best – one, and the house was a small two-bedroomed bungalow.

They opened the door to the kitchen and their eyes lit up. Sat there in the middle of the table was a roast chicken that Viv must have cooked before she went to bed.

"Just nice," Lewis had said, as he looked around for the cutlery drawer. When he turned back to ask Cliff if he knew where the knives and forks were kept, he was greeted with the sight of him holding the full chicken up to his mouth and taking a massive bite out of the breast. According to Lewis, as he put it down on the table, he looked like Henry the Eighth's little brother.

Lewis had whispered, "You bloody idiot, you can't do that, they'll know now," as if they wouldn't have known anyway, because it was hardly a bowl of soup. So Lewis

---

[22] Ears

picked up the chicken and nibbled around Cliff's teeth marks, explaining that he was tidying it up so Vera and Stan wouldn't find out.

For years, they thought that Stan and Vera didn't know, until they were a lot older and had a night telling stories at home. Maisie had told them that Vera and Stan were lying in bed listening to the two of them, trying to stifle their laughs. They said they hadn't the heart to say anything the next day.

"Well, she's gone now," I said, "let's have a drink on Viv."

We nodded and touched our Tuborgs together.

Vera's death had come as quite a shock to us. We knew she was ill, but we thought that it was only an ulcer on her leg. I suppose we didn't really take it in, more concerned with other things going on in our lives. Apparently, Vera was diabetic, and when she got the ulcer on her leg, the doctors couldn't do anything about it, so they had to amputate. It seemed that she had given up a couple of days after the amputation. I found it hard to believe, because I knew the kind of woman she and, by extension, my Mam were.

At dinner, we ordered a chateau brieaund, which was the most expensive meal on the menu. Johansens were paying for the hotel, and we reasoned that it was only fair compensation for the messing about we had put up with. I don't think either of us was in the mood for staying downstairs and womanising the waitress, so we made our way back to my room to ring Mam.

When we got there, Lewis asked if I had brought a bottle of scotch with me. I told him where it was and we decided to open it and have another quick drink on Vera.

I picked up the phone and typed in the necessary international code and Maisie's number. As I waited for it to connect, I took a sip of the large whisky Lewis had poured out for me. I looked over to him, holding the glass up in an enquiring sort of manner. Lewis held his up and winked at me.

"Hello?" Maisie answered the phone.

"Alreet, Mam? We've just heard about Viv."

"I know. I only found out today. Stan didn't want anyone to know," she said, beginning to sob.

I turned to Lewis, gesturing that Mam was crying.

She told me that the funeral was in two days' time, and she wouldn't be able to go because she couldn't get there. But we were adamant that Maisie would be going to her sister's funeral. We told her that she had to go and say her goodbyes properly, because otherwise she would never forgive herself. If we hadn't been stuck in Denmark, either one of us could have driven her to Cornwall, but as ironic as life likes to be, we were over a thousand miles away. As luck would have it, Cliff was in the house, and we arranged for him to ring his boss, who was a very understanding chap, and ask for the time off to take Maisie to Cornwall.

We must have been on the phone for over two hours, and in that time we had drunk one and a half litres of Glenmorangie malt whisky. By the time we hung up, it was nearly one o'clock in the morning and we had to be up in six hours.

It was upsetting, talking to Mam on the phone, because we had never heard her crying and being so negative about things. I don't think we appreciated the fact that Vera was Maisie's only blood relation left, apart from us kids, of course, but that was different. We ourselves had never experienced a death in the family, because our grandparents had either died before we were born, or when we were too young to remember.

It was a strange night. But the underlying thought was that when we needed Maisie, she was always there for us, and the only time she needed us, we couldn't be at home for her.

Whisky Breath

The next morning, I felt as rough as a brush. I phoned Lewis's room to wake him up, but he didn't answer.

Surely, he couldn't have gone missing again?

"'Ello?" He croaked.

"Bloody 'ell, you sound as rough as I feel."

"Oh yeah, after I went back to my room last night I got in bed and the room started to spin."

"Oh no, you weren't sick?"

"I was."

"Where?"

"All over the floor."

"Oh, fuckin' 'ell Lewis. Well, you better get it tidied up, you scruffy bleeder."

"Calm down, calm down," he said in a Liverpool accent, "I'm only jokin'."

"What, you weren't sick then?"

"Oh aye, I were sick alright, but it's in the bog[23]."

"Well, get your arse out of bed and let's get some breakfast. Peter'll be here for us in forty-five minutes." I put the phone down.

---

[23] Toilet

I half expected to see our receptionist/barmaid from last night, but like most hotels, the morning staff were different from the evening staff – even the guests looked different.

Lewis came into the dining area looking every bit as rough as he had sounded on the phone.

Serves him right, he was the one who kept tippin' the whisky out last night.

'Oh we'll just have another.' Payin' for it now.

"Oh, I'm never touchin' that shit again," he slumped into the chair beside me.

"Well, you kept tippin' them out."

"And you, I've supped about half a gallon of water this mornin', and cleaned me teeth three times, but I can't get rid of that bloody awful taste."

"You won't do, kid. I remember when I was sick on whisky! It's not like beer, it'll take a couple of days to wear off."

"I don't wanna full 'un."

"Good job, 'cause it's only ham, cheese, and bread."

"Good, might soak some of this whisky up."

I could fully appreciate how Lewis was feeling, because I felt terrible too. But at least I hadn't been sick. I really wasn't looking forward to loading the rest of the trees.

We returned back to our rooms to finish packing our bits and in Lewis' case, brushing his teeth another couple of times, and then we went outside to wait for Peter with about ten minutes or so before he was due to arrive.

It was as cold a morning as all the rest had been, but apart from the hangovers, we were better prepared to tackle it, because we hadn't spent the night cooped up in a box on wheels. The sun was rising, and there wasn't a cloud in the sky. It was a beautiful day.

After about twenty minutes, Peter showed up apologising for being late and remarking on how we both looked. I told him we had a few drinks, but I spared him the story of our Aunt because he didn't need to know, and anyway, most people don't know what to say when faced with a situation like that, so I spared him the details.

When we arrived at the farm, it seemed different than it did the previous day. I didn't know why, perhaps I didn't notice much about it yesterday.

The trees and truck were still where we had left them last night, and the men were in the farmyard doing their chores. Essentially, it was a pig farm.

Before we started to load the trees, the guys who worked on the farm decided to take a break. I thought that I might have been able to squeeze in another brew and perhaps a bacon sarnie. I couldn't have been more wrong. The guys all had bottles of juice, and they ate either Rugbrød (rye bread) or Danish pastries. It seemed rather strange to me, but then, who was I to judge, a greasy Full English is hardly health food. Lewis couldn't get over the fact that not one of them had a thermos flask, but they just didn't do cups of tea or coffee.

When the guys had finished their break and our customary questions on women and football had been answered, we went outside and started to load the trees. Once we started it was obvious that our hearts weren't in the job at all, due to a combination of whisky, grief, and the fact that we were impatient to get loaded up and get home.

"What about this one, Bert?" Lewis asked.

"Oh, just throw it on."

"I thought we were gradin' them?"

"Fuck 'em. Even if we spend all day goin' through them, when we get back Dougal Arse'll only find fault anyway, so fuck 'em."

We loaded the trees as they came. There wasn't a bad mix of them actually. It's strange when you sell trees to the public, because they don't all want big bushy ones, some even want them with one side missing, so it will sit tight into a corner, others snap the tops off, there were all kinds of strange requests. If we all liked the same things, we would all be chasing the same woman.

After we had loaded and secured the trees, the farmer took us on a tour of his farm, not that by this time we really wanted to, but we felt obliged because he had been such a nice guy.

When the tour was over, we said our goodbyes for the final time to Peter and the other workers, and jumped back into the truck. It was only one o'clock, so I anticipated being back at Johansens in about three hours, just before it got dark. We would have to sort out the necessary paperwork and then we'd finally be getting rid of the bloody money in the briefcase. I hoped we could perhaps get as far south as Hamburg before parking up for the night.

I probably shouldn't have been driving until the next day, because I still felt drunk.

What the hell.

Surely not much more can go wrong on this trip.

Right?

Oh No - Edith!

We were making good time as we joined the motorway on Fyn. Lewis was busy gabbing away about something and I was daydreaming a bit myself, when I could make out a bridge looming ahead of us.

"Hey, that bugger looks low."

"It'll be reet," I reassured Lewis, although I wasn't that sure. I had seen trucks on the other side with the same type of trailer on, and I thought that they must have come under it, so I just kept my foot hard down on the accelerator. The mood I was in, I couldn't care less.

"Slow down, you bloody idiot!" wailed Lewis as the bridge rapidly approached. I began to wonder if he was right.

As we got to the bridge, Lewis ducked down, holding his head and I shut my eyes. There was a scraping noise, and we popped out of the other side. I looked in the mirrors and everything looked fine. Lewis raised his head and I starting bragging, saying that I knew all along that it would be alright. "Bollocks, we hit that bugger."

"The sheet just scraped on it."

"Bloody good job it wasn't a few inches higher, else we would've hit it."

"Stop whingin' – we were miles away," I laughed.

"Don't do that again, you frightened me to bloody death, you nobhead."

I had to admit, I gave myself a fright.

We had been driving quite happily for about an hour and a half, when my earlier thoughts of nothing else going wrong came back to haunt me.

"Oh no," I muttered, tapping at the dash.

"What's up?"

"Bloody alternator light's come on."

"What does that mean?"

"Well, either the drive-belt's snapped, which is highly unlikely, 'cause I put new ones on last week, or the alternator's knackered."

"So, what does that mean?"

"We'll have to get it fixed, 'cause all it's doin' now is runnin' the batteries down, and with us havin' to have the lights on durin' the day, and the heater to keep us warm, that won't take long."

"Will the truck stop?"

"No, with it being diesel and not petrol, it dun't need a spark to ignite the fuel, so the truck won't stop, but we won't have any electric to work the lights, heater, or start the bugger."

"We'll have to ask Dan. They must know somewhere to get it fixed."

We arrived at Johansens' yard about an hour later. I left the engine running as we went up to the offices. The lights on the truck were barely visible - the battery must have been nearly flat. The yard itself was busier than before. When we got into the office, there were people all over. It was organised chaos.

Dan acknowledged us and shouted over from his workstation for us to go into the little canteen area that we had been to on our previous visit. We went in and sat down but as we did so, a girl came in and asked us if we would like coffee or tea.

"Oh, tea please," I said, not having had a cup of tea for a long while.

"I like tea also," she said, with a slight accent. "Everybody in Denmark seems to prefer coffee."

"We haven't had a decent brew all the time we've been here," said Lewis. She just looked at him, probably trying to work out what he had just said.

"He means tea," I explained.

"Oh, hello. She's off again," he said sarcastically.

"Shuddup," I smirked.

"Right," Dan rushed through the open doorway. "How was your loading? Everything okay? Do you like the trees?" He didn't wait for an answer, he just carried on talking about how busy they were and how he liked England, London, and – strangely enough – Newcastle Brown Ale.

"Can we sort out the money, Dan?" I asked. "'Cause I wanna get rid of it. It's been nothin' but a bloody nuisance."

"Oh, Jack, you could have left the money in the vault here, it would have been most safe."

Lewis and I looked at each other.

Dan produced his invoice, the necessary T2 form, and health certificate for the trees, to prove that they had come from a disease-free area. We counted out the money – eight thousand three hundred and twenty pounds - with a hundred and twenty pounds off for luck money, making it eight thousand two hundred pounds. The remaining one thousand eight hundred pounds would be enough to cover customs and excise - or as it's more commonly known, VAT - when we docked in the UK.

For some reason, Dan was intrigued with the Barclays money bag, and asked if he could keep it. I agreed, since we had no further use for it, and told him about our problem with the truck. He assured us that we had no problem, as they had an account with a Mercedes truck garage in Padborg. He left the room with the money in the

Barclays bag.

When he returned, he told me that he had phoned the service centre at the Mercedes garage and they were expecting us. He also gave us directions and a few complimentary Johansens umbrellas. I've no idea why, but we took them anyway. We bid Dan and the other guys in the office a fond farewell, thanked them for their hospitality, and left the offices, heading outside to the still-running truck.

Can You Fix It?

Eventually, we found the Mercedes garage. It was quite a new, modern-looking building which appeared closed at first glance, but I noticed a guy through the big glass doors. I parked the truck and walked over to the doors where I had seen him.

I pulled and pushed at the doors, but they were locked. So I banged on them. I couldn't see anybody there now, so I shouted, "Hello, hello?" Suddenly, a bald-headed guy with a little goatee came to the door and said something in Danish or German. I couldn't understand him. "Dan Johansen's sent us to get our truck repaired." He looked right through me.

This bugger doesn't know anythin' about it.

"Johansens? Dan Johansen." I shouted through the doors.

"Ah, yes," he finally understood me. He opened the doors and instructed me to go through a set of gates, which he would open, and to the rear of the service bays to drop the trailer, where somebody would deal with us.

'Deal with us' – sounds like we've done somethin' wrong.

We went to the big steel gates and they opened automatically. We drove around the back of the garage and

172

dropped the trailer. I manoeuvred the tractor unit to the front of the garage doors, ready to be summoned in when they opened.

It was well lit outside on the concrete apron. We could see into the garage because they had vision panels in the big roller-shutter doors. I could see trucks on the other side of the doors, but no people. Slowly, faces began to appear at the vision panels, staring at us. Within a few minutes, we must have had everybody in the place looking through the windows. It was a bit unnerving.

Lewis shouted, "What's up? Have you never seen a proper truck before?"

"That's probably what's wrong, 'cause when I was tellin' the guy at the front what kind of truck it was, he just stared at me. So they've probably come to have a look."

The door started moving up and the guys reversed a truck out to make room for us. When it was safely out of the way, someone motioned us forward, so I steered into the bay.

Before we climbed down from the cab, we stashed everything away; bags, cooker, beer - so it didn't come crashing through the windscreen. I tipped the cab up for the mechanic we had been allotted, and tried to explain the problem to him. The other mechanics were having a sneaky peak all the time we were there, as well as trying to get on with their own work, which was wholly on brand new trucks. I couldn't help thinking that the mechanics had drawn straws, and the guy who was dealing with us had got the short one.

I had to admit, our truck did look like a bit of a scrap heap in the middle of all those new Mercedes trucks, but it was *our* scrap heap, and it had to get us back to the UK.

I explained to the mechanic that the alternator had gone wrong and it needed a new one, but he couldn't speak English and I couldn't speak Danish.

He went for help.

After a few minutes, we had a couple more mechanics

with us, and it transpired that they called an alternator a generator, and they couldn't have fixed it there anyway, as all they had were Mercedes parts. But they were going to send us to an auto electrician in Padborg who could help us.

We put the cab back down, sorted our stuff out, and, armed with fresh directions, hitched up the trailer and set off looking for the auto electrician. They had assured us that they would be there, as they had phoned to tell them we were on our way.

We found the auto electrician quite easily, and the guys were waiting for us. It was a smaller, much friendlier sort of place than the Mercedes garage had been, not that the guys weren't friendly, but it had a no-nonsense, clinical feel about it.

We dropped the trailer on a huge, communal car park and drove into the garage. After we had tipped the cab, I explained to the guys how the generator had gone wrong and we needed a new one. Without a moment's hesitation, they set to work and took off the old generator. After about five minutes or so, talking amongst themselves, they told us that they didn't have anything like our generator, but they would try their best to fit us up with something. They then disappeared into the back, while Lewis and I wondered where we were going to spend the night. We went outside to have a cigarette while we waited.

"Hey, when we were in that hotel last night, did you put the telly on?" Lewis asked.

"No, why?"

"Well, when I got in the room, I switched everythin' on like you do, and I was havin' a look 'round on the telly and I came across a German porno channel."

"Bollocks!"

"No, honest. It was a good story as well, there was this housewife who opened her front door to a policeman –

next news, he's takin' her from behind in the kitchen. I thought, bloody 'ell, it's only about half six at night. That was one of the reasons I was ringin' you, to tell you to put it on."

"Proper porno at that time of night?"

"Yeah, honest!"

"Bollocks! Knowin' you, you probably accessed a pay porno channel."

"I'm tellin' you, it was on normal telly. Better than bloody *Emmerdale Farm* anyway," laughed Lewis.

"Aye, can you imagine Seth Armstrong rattlin' Annie Sugden? Put you off your tea," I laughed.

As we were laughing, the guy in charge came out to have a word with us.

"This doesn't look good," I said.

"I can put a new generator on, but it will be off a Wolwo, and also I need to take parts off your old one," the mechanic said.

"A what?" I asked, "Wolwo, what's a Wolwo?"

"Yes, Wolwo," he repeated, "a Wolwo truck."

"Oh," the penny dropped. "A Volvo."

"Yes, a Wolwo." The Danes pronounced v's as w's.

"Well, please do whatever's necessary to get us on the road. Will it be fixed tonight?"

"We will try our best."

And, to be honest, I believed him. They were good guys. Two of them stayed until about half past nine working on the truck to get us going. When we dropped the cab back down we had to jump-start the truck, because the batteries were flat. We celebrated by giving the guys two six-packs of Grolsch. It was obvious that they hadn't seen the brew before, because they thought it was English.

We signed for the work the guys had done and set off for customs. As we knew the procedure now, we simply did everything we did when we entered Denmark a few days ago, but in reverse. All the paperwork seemed to be in order, and I exchanged the Danish Kroner we had left over to German Deutchmarks, and we were soon on our way back home.

We drove for a couple of hours, which took us to the outskirts of Hamburg. It was enough driving to be getting on with for the time being, I thought. It had been a long day, and was also a decent test for the alternator. It was behaving, so they must have done a good job. Also, it was just enough distance travelled to charge the batteries back up.

We pulled into the services, half expecting there to be no parking spaces, but to our amazement it was empty. We soon got parked up, but we were so tired that we couldn't be bothered going into the services for anything to eat. So we readied the cab, assumed our sleeping positions, and must have been asleep within about five minutes of settling down.

"Ziehen. Sie Vorbei!"

The next morning, we felt much better than we had done the previous day. We went into the services, had a quick wash, and devoured the continental breakfast that we were getting used to by now. As we finished our coffee, Lewis asked how much German money we had.

"Why?"

"Well, there looks like there's some cheap beer in the shop here, and after you give them two Arnie's some of our Grolsch, we're runnin' out."

"Here," I handed him some of the German money we had. Lewis took it and disappeared into the shop. He came out a few minutes later with a case of DAB lager. I had never heard of it, and neither had Lewis, but he assured me that it looked like good stuff.

Back at the truck, Lewis loaded his shopping while I did the checks around the truck. Everything okay, apart from a couple of the ropes securing the trees, which had come loose due to settlement. After re-securing the ropes, I climbed into the cab and, fingers crossed, turned the key. The engine seemed to turn very slowly for a split second, and then-

Vroom!

"The old bastard's teasin' us now, Lewis."

"Well, it's fucked us about enough, so I suppose teasin' in't too bad."

We set off out of the services towards Hamburg. The traffic was quite heavy, it was as if the whole of Denmark was heading south. As we got closer to the centre of Hamburg on the motorway network, we started to see signs for the Elb tunnel.

We approached the entrances to the tunnel, and I could see that there were two available southbound and one northbound, obviously because of the volume of traffic travelling southbound.

Suddenly, massive illuminated signs above the lanes lit up with flashing red lights saying 'STOP'. If the cars in front of us hadn't stopped, I would have sailed straight into the tunnel. As everybody came to a halt, we looked around, trying to see what the problem was.

"Hey up," said Lewis, "look up there." He pointed over at a slip road that joined the carriageway. "There's an ambulance comin' down, somebody must've been run over in the tunnel."

"That's not an ambulance, you pillock, it's a police van."

"Is it? Looks like an ambulance to me."

The police van reversed down the exit lane and into the centre of the lanes, the doors opened and two policemen got out. With their green uniforms and leather-bound hats, they looked like they meant business. They both started to move the traffic on and the warning lights went off.

"What was all that about then?" I looked over at Lewis, who looked just as puzzled as I felt.

The cars in front of us began to move, so I set off behind them. Driving up to the policemen, they motioned us towards the hard shoulder.

"Ziehen. Sie vorbei!"

"Who's he pointin' at?"

"I don't know," I replied, looking in the mirrors to see

if there was a problem behind.

"Bloody 'ell, it's us!" The policeman moved closer and pointed straight at us, and gestured towards the hard shoulder again.

"Ziehen. Sie vorbei!"

"Tell me the truth, did you pay for them beers this mornin' or did you nick them?"

"I paid for them."

"Well, you must've nicked summat."

"I've nicked fuck all!"

"Well, what do these buggers want us for, then?"

"I dunno, it's nowt to do with me."

I pulled the truck over to the hard shoulder as instructed by the older of the two German policemen, the younger one then came over to Lewis' side of the truck and started shouting something in German and pointing to the top of the trailer.

Lewis shrugged his shoulders at the policemen and pointed at me, making a motion like someone driving. The policeman came around to my side of the truck and set about shouting at me and pointing to the top of the trailer, as he had done with Lewis. Then the older policeman came to the driver's side of the truck and said something to the younger guy, who immediately went off to the van they had both arrived in.

The older guy looked quite scruffy for a policeman. He looked as though he needed a shave, and his uniform appeared to be made for a bigger guy altogether.

First up, best dressed eh?

"Fuhrershein bitte."

"Sorry, what?"

"Fuhrerschein, Fuhrerschein," he demanded, getting a little excited.

Floorshine? What the fuck does floorshine mean?

As I looked down on him, wondering what he wanted, I couldn't help thinking that he was a dead ringer for Albert Steptoe, of *Steptoe and Son*. We had been accosted by the German version of Albert and his downtrodden son, Harold.

"Fuhrerschein," he said again, making a driving gesture with his hands.

"Ah, driving licence?" I asked.

"Ja, Ja, drive licence."

I rummaged around in my bag to find my driving licence and handed it over to Albert. He studied it, shaking his head.

Fuck me, what's wrong with him now? And why the hell have they pulled us over?

"Das ist nicht gut, es ist keine richtige fuhrerschein," he said, passing my licence back to me.

A no good floorshine? You cheeky bugger, my licence is a good floorshine.

I stepped down out of the truck to talk face to face with Albert. He wasn't a very tall man, and he straightened up slightly to make himself appear taller as I approached him. I towered over him by at least a foot, he must have felt the same way as I did when I was amongst the trolls the other day.

Plastic card licences had been in use for several years on the continent, so Albert mustn't have recognised my paper one as a driving licence, or indeed any proof of ID.

"Ah! What about my passport? Will my passport do you?"

"Ja, reisepass ist gut,holen Sie es bitte fur mich."

"What does he want? One of our Bitters?" joked Lewis, as I climbed back into the cab.

"Shut up, you nobhead, and go see what Harold's doing."

"Harold?"

"Yeah Harold fuckin' Steptoe, his mate."

"Fuck me yeah, he does look like Albert Steptoe doesn't he? The scruffy old bastard!" giggled Lewis.

I handed my passport over to Albert. While he was studying it, I looked around to see Lewis standing with

Harold, who was holding some sort of collapsible stick at the side of the trailer whilst talking to Lewis. Lewis was nodding his head in a very understanding and knowing manner.

Harold must speak English, at least we can find out what the problem is.

"Das ist gut," said Albert, handing back my passport.

Harold and Lewis joined us at the front of the truck. Albert took Harold to one side, probably to talk about my rubbish floorshine.

"So, what's the problem?" I asked Lewis.

"Fucked if I know."

"What do you mean, 'Fucked if you know'? I saw you talkin' to Harold, you were noddin' your head and everythin'."

"Yeah I know, but I still don't know what the fuck he said. I think the trailer's too high or summat."

"Too high? We came this way into Denmark and it's the same fuckin' trailer!"

I looked at the trailer and it dawned on me, we had folded up the huge cover that normally envelopes the trailer sides into a nice little bed at the front of the trailer, to make loading easier. As we had been driving, wind had got underneath the pleats and lifted it slightly, not that it would have done any damage to the bridge, but it was nevertheless high enough to activate the sensors and send *Steptoe and Son* to investigate. Albert and Harold wandered back to us.

"Ihr wagen ist Einhundert Zentimeter zu hoch, braucht Sie mussen es niedriger," said Albert as he approached us, pointing towards Big Edith.

"Too high? Is that what you're sayin' Albert?"

"Ja, ja, too high," chirped Harold, obviously Albert's translator. "Einhundert Zentimetre."

"What's ine?" I said, turning to Lewis. "That's one, innit? So that's one hundred centimetres too high, that's four inches. Four fuckin' inches too high! Fuck me, Albert, you can't do us for bein' just four inches too high, surely?"

Albert looked up at me and pointed to Big Edith again, "Niedrigere, Niedrigere."

"Think he wants us to tie the sheet back down," said Lewis.

"No shit, Sherlock," I replied sarcastically.

"Hey! Don't have a go at me, it's not my fuckin' fault!"

Lewis and I got the spare ropes from the back of the trailer and secured the sheet down at the front. Harold measured it again and nodded his satisfaction to Albert, who then gestured for me to follow him to the police van.

It was lovely and warm in the back of the van, which had bench seats and a little table in between them. Albert and I sat opposite each other. He removed his cap, took out a piece of paper from a little pigeon hole to his left, and started to write on it. When he had finished what he was doing, he looked up at me.

"Ihr fahrzeug wurde uber die zulassige Hohe den tunnel eingeben-"

Albert, I don't understand a fuckin word you're sayin'!

I tried to look interested, though.

Come on, get the bollockin' over with, then we can get goin'.

"-Nachdem Sie das problem behoben haben freuen wir uns, dass fortfahren konnen, aber du must eine geldbuBe-"

Yeah, yeah, c'mon get on with it!

"-von zweihundert deutchmarks zu bezahlen , bevor wir dich gehen lassen-"

Deutchmarks?

Did he just say fuckin' Deutchmarks?

"Sorry Albert, I haven't a clue what you just said."

"Was? Wer ist Albert? Mein name ist Helmut."

"Sorry Helmet , but I-"

"Ist Helmut, Nicht Helmet," he said angrily, turning to the pigeon holes on his left again, this time withdrawing another document which he placed on the table in front of me. "Bitte lessen Sie diese englischen mann," he spat.

The document that Albert had put in front of me quite

clearly stated – in many languages, including good old English – that if we did not pay the two hundred Deutchmark fine, we could find ourselves in prison, and the truck impounded with a parking charge of one hundred Deutchmarks per day until the fine is paid. Reluctantly, I paid the fine. As I put the money in his grubby little hand, I asked, "Do I get a receipt?"

"Was?" he said, whilst counting the money.

"Receipt, for the money?"

He looked up from the table and pointed toward the door of the police van. "Sie konnen jetzt gehen."

"What? I can go? What about a receipt?"

"Gehen," he said again.

Beer money is it Albert? Nice little earner for you, you Teutonic twat. Buy a new uniform, get a shave, and have a bath.

I got back into the truck, and Lewis was already sat there. I started Big Edith's engine, slipped her into gear, and made my way back into the morning traffic heading south.

"Well?"

"Two hundred bastard Deutchmarks."

"What for?"

"'Cause we were too high."

"Bollocks," said Lewis, "there've been plenty go past higher than us. Anyway, I'm not sure it *was* us that set that bloody sensor off."

"No, I'm not either, but if we hadn't paid we were gonna end up in the nick."

"Dougal Arse would've liked that. Ah well, could've been worse."

"How?"

"They could've pulled us yesterday when we were still pissed."

"Aye, if that alternator hadn't broken down, they would've done."

"Oh well, never mind, eh. Anyway, how much money have we got left?"

"Buggered if I know, but it won't be much 'cause that fine was about seventy quid, why?"

"Well, we need to look out for a supermarket."

"Supermarket?" I asked, confused.

"Yeah, 'cause I need some new undies, these I've got on need throwin' out."

"Them aren't still the same ones from Belgium, are they?"

"Yeah."

"Maisie won't be pleased when she finds out you only brought two pairs."

"She won't know."

"Anyway, what's the problem? They'll do you 'til we get home."

"I know, but what if we come across Celine again in Belgium?"

"Oh, now we're gettin' to it. I thought there had to be a good reason for you goin' all hygienic," I laughed.

"Well, you never know."

"You're bloody right there, the way things are goin', anythin' could happen."

"Stop whingin' – it can't get any worse," Lewis said, passing me a Gitane.

"It just has, I thought we'd smoked all these buggers!"

New Undies

The German countryside flew past as we made our way steadily south towards Venlo. The mood in the cab was slightly more upbeat than it had been on the way up to Denmark, mainly because we were going home and the truck had been behaving itself.

"In't it somewhere 'round here where that fancy toilet was?"

"Probably," I replied, "to be honest, I can't really remember. Why, do you need to stop?"

"No, I'm alreet, I was just thinkin' out loud. Hey – look!" He pointed at something in the distance.

"What?"

"On the right up there, aren't they tanks?"

When I looked into the distance, I could make out a convoy of about ten military tanks. I couldn't tell whether they were British, German, or what, but they were certainly moving at some pace. They must have been on a dirt track, because as we got closer I could see that they were throwing mud up behind them.

As we were catching up to them, they turned left onto a motorway bridge in front of us. It was very impressive to see these machines trundling over the bridge. We looked on in awe and the front tank slewed its turret around. It seemed as though it were pointing straight at us.

"Fuckin' 'ell," I laughed, "you haven't upset the army as well, have you?"

It was quite unnerving to have a huge gun barrel pointing at us. Once we passed under the bridge, I felt a slight sense of relief.

You daft bugger, as if they're gonna shoot at you.

"Hey, bit airy[24] that, Bert."

"Aye, I wonder where they're off to."

"If they were English, probably home for a brew."

It was nearly time for us to take a break and Lewis said that he wanted to go shopping. I told him it wasn't that easy, as we weren't driving round in a bloody Mini.

"Ah, we'll find somewhere to park, kid," said Lewis confidently. "Here we are, Bert. Can we pull off here?"

"Why here?"

"There, look – a supermarket," he pointed at a building looming on the left-hand side of the autobahn.

"Where?" I asked, looking in the direction Lewis had been pointing.

"There, it's an Asda."

"Asda? That says Aldi."

"That's just German for Asda," he said knowledgeably.

"How the hell d'you work that one out?"

"It's reet, I'm tellin' you."

I put the indicator on and pulled onto the slip road to leave the autobahn.

What the bloody hell are you doing, Bert?

The supermarket proved quite easy to get to, we turned into the entrance and made our way around the car park to find a suitable parking spot. And fair play to Lewis, it *was* a supermarket, because the usual giveaway signs were there for all to see, like the trolleys.

Needless to say, we raised a few eyebrows as we drove

---

[24] Scary

around the car park. Hardly surprising really, when you go for your pint of milk and sauerkraut, you don't expect to see two English guys riding around the car park in an articulated truck loaded with Christmas trees.

"C'mon, our kid," Lewis eagerly jumped down out of the truck.

"Calm down, I don't think they're gonna sell out of undies."

Walking through the door, it didn't seem any different to Asda, although the signs were a different colour.

"Hey, don't be nickin' 'owt."

"I won't." Lewis walked off down the aisle to one of the staff who was stacking shelves. "'Scuse me love, d'you sell undies?"

"Bitte," she said.

"Bitter? No, undies," said Lewis, turning to me, smiling.

"Stop pissin' about," I told him, under my breath. "He needs underwear," I said, making a circular motion around my hips with my fingers, in a vain attempt to describe what I meant. She looked at me in confusion.

So Lewis, with his obvious flare for bridging the language barrier, decided he would take over. "I need some new undies," he said, pointing vigorously at his crotch area.

"Ah," the assistant said with a knowing smile, and she steered us to another section of the supermarket.

"Nowt to it, kid. Should've been an interpreter, me."

We caught up to the assistant and she reached up on a shelf, offering Lewis a small box.

"Won't be reet big undies in there, Lewis." He took the box from the woman and read it.

"*Prolificatos*? What does that mean?"

"They're bloody condoms!" I laughed. "I bet she thinks we're gay!"

"No, no," Lewis said, as he passed the pack of condoms back to the assistant, whose face dropped in disappointment. She must have thought that she'd finally worked out what we wanted.

"I want new undies," said Lewis, pulling his trousers open at the top to reveal his underpants.

"Hey, go steady! You can't do that in here, you'll get us locked up!"

"Well, how'm I gonna explain what I want?"

"You were just tellin' me how easy it was a minute ago, all this foreign language stuff," I laughed.

"Piss off! You know what I mean."

"Hold on, I think you're in luck. She wants us to go over there." I pointed to the aisle where the woman had gone to after Lewis' little show of exhibitionism.

To be honest, the assistant didn't even bat an eyelid when Lewis started dropping his trousers.

Perhaps it's all them porno films they have here.

"Okay?" she asked, as she passed Lewis a much larger box this time.

I had to walk away laughing, because she had given Lewis a packet of washing powder – she must have thought he wanted to wash them!

"I don't wanna wash me undies! I just want bloody new ones," said Lewis, obviously getting frustrated now.

"Hey, calm down kid," I said, laughing. "It's not her fault that she doesn't understand your German."

At this, the woman walked away in the direction of the tills.

"We're in trouble now, she'll have gone for a manager to throw us out."

"Why? We haven't done 'owt."

"Only jokin' kid, I think she's gone for help."

She returned with a guy in a suit. "Can I help you?"

"Yeah, I want some new undies." Lewis explained.

"New undies?" repeated the guy, with a puzzled look on his face. "What is new undies?"

"Er – I mean underwear."

"Ah, yes. Follow me, please." He marched off in the

opposite direction and I thought that we might stand a chance this time. He took us to the clothing section and left us to it.

"Here you are, kid," I held up a pair of knickers that were big enough for the both of us to get into.

"Shuddup," he laughed. "They'd even be too big for Maisie, them."

He eventually decided on a pair of boxer shorts.

"Bit flash for you them, aren't they?"

"Hey, just nice for me, these." He held them to his side and looked up at me, grinning. "I wonder if they'll let me try them on?"

"You what? They wouldn't let *you* try a belt on, you scruffy sod."

We paid for Lewis's new underwear, but not before we had a good look around at the products on sale. We tried to see if there was anything we recognised, like baked beans, biscuits, or anything like that. We couldn't find any brands that we had heard of before, so ignorantly, we made our minds up that the products on sale couldn't have been that good.

I hoped that when we got back to the truck, we could make a swift cup of tea and then get going, but the truck had generated a bit of interest with the local shoppers and, worst of all, a traffic warden.

Amazingly, he was a really nice guy. He asked us where in the UK we were from, and when we said Manchester, he started talking about Manchester United Football Club.

How ironic, this guy can speak perfect English and he wants to talk to Lewis about a football club he hates.

Lewis was a Liverpool fan, so I made our excuses to get out of there fast, because I knew that once Lewis started to get excited about his beloved Liverpool, we could end up with a load of parking tickets. Or worse, in jail. Having already dodged it once today, I thought it was best that we forgot about the tea.

"Are you puttin' your new undies on, then?" I pulled

out of the supermarket and onto the autobahn.

"Am I 'eck. These are me new best undies now." He was smug about it. "So I'm gonna save them 'til we get to Belgium."

"We might not even see Celine."

"It don't matter. We'll find summat, we might even get you a jump."

"Aye, perhaps I should've bought some new undies then!" I laughed.

It was about five o'clock in the evening when we pulled into the transit lane at the German/Dutch border of Venlo. We were coasting up to the elevated kiosk to customs, when we noticed a guy waving us through. It looked like he wasn't interested in our paperwork.

You'll do for me.

I slipped the truck into gear and drove out of the transit lane and into the service area.

"Well, that was easy enough."

"Aye, easier than I thought it'd be. Right then Lewis, let's get summat to eat and a few beers, our kid."

"Summat to eat? Tell you what, I never thought I'd miss the chippy."

"Oh aye – pie, chips, peas, and a couple of slices of Warburtons bread."

"No! Puddin', chips and gravy. Mmm." Lewis licked his lips.

"Shuddup, you're makin' me hungrier than ever."

"Or one of Maisie's bacon sarnies… Mmm."

"No, one of Maisie's full 'un's."

"Oh aye, a bloody full 'un." Lewis rolled his eyes skyward.

"Well, stop dreamin'. At the best, you're havin' a shit sausage."

It was quite an uneventful night. We got some lovely Dutch cuisine, and although I didn't know what it was, I think it had mincemeat in it somewhere. It was alright but, as Lewis kept saying, it wasn't a chippy dinner.

We had a few drinks in the cab and discussed major topics, like what time we might get home on Saturday, and where we would go for a drink when we got there. It felt as though we had been away for weeks, but it was only a few days. It was a lot more pleasant than it had been in the cab, not just because I had stopped farting, but because the weather had turned much milder, and the temperature was in double figures for a change.

Before we went to sleep we planned the rest of our trip home. When we got to Ostend, we'd book the next morning's ferry, leave the truck on the dock, get rooms at the Hotel Marion and go on the hunt for the girls, Monique and Celine.

Well, that was the plan anyway.

Ostend Strike

The next morning we had a bit of a lie in instead of getting ready and setting off, like we had been doing for the past few days. It was only about a four or five hour drive back to Ostend, so we reasoned that we would be there with plenty of time to sort things out.

I had to admit, the roads in Holland and Belgium were far superior to the ones we had driven on in northern Germany, and having said that, the UK too. We were making good time as we went through the transit lane at the Dutch/Belgian border at Turnhout, so we parked up to take a break and have a cup of coffee. I hoped that we would be back in Ostend by about five o'clock.

I was feeling rather good now, because apart from the ticket office on the docks at Ostend, the one we had just gone through was the last customs office on the continent – the next one would be at Dover.

After our coffee and a couple of Gitanes, we got going again, but it wasn't long before we had to stop. We hit a traffic jam just outside Gent. It wasn't the kind of traffic that slowly moves forward either, it was the kind in which you just stay still. We were stuck in the same spot for over three hours.

Eventually we started moving, and within half an hour we had passed the trouble. While we were sitting in the queue, we had been guessing what might have happened – road works, broken down car, accident, we wondered what form our hold-up would come in. As we drove past the scene, it turned out that it was a car transporter, full of cars, and it had been on fire.

"Cocked us up, that."

"What d'you mean?"

"Well, we aren't gonna be in Ostend now 'til about nine o'clock, and by the time we've checked in on the docks, it'll be about ten," I moaned.

"So? We can still go out for a few."

"Aye, if we can get in anywhere."

We arrived in Ostend, as I predicted, at ten past nine but it was completely shrouded in thick fog, which must have been because of the weather warming up slightly, or maybe sea mist. Either way, it made Ostend feel like a different place from the one to which we had arrived. We negotiated our way to the docks only to find that the massive, ornate, wrought-iron entrance gates were closed.

We sat there, wondering if it was too late and if the gates would be shut for the night, when a guy appeared out of a little office to the side of the gates and handed us a leaflet. The leaflet was printed in various European languages. I looked down until I found the English version and read that the docks were shut because the workers had gone on strike for a twenty-four hour period, ending at six o'clock in the morning.

"Bloody 'ell, that's all we need," I said, throwing the piece of paper to Lewis for his perusal.

I jumped down out of the truck and went over to the office where the guy had appeared from, and asked him if it was possible to leave the truck in the safety of the docks. He said that he was very sorry but we couldn't. He informed us that the Calais/Dover ferries were still running, so that was where all the other freight had gone to, because if your ticket was with P&O ferries it was redeemable at Calais. I explained that we didn't have enough driving hours to get to Calais, and asked if it would be possible to park at the side of the marina. He said that would be fine, and he would try to keep an eye on it for us.

"Right," I returned to the truck. "He said we can park near the marina, but he doesn't think we'll get in a hotel, 'cause of the strike. It's a Friday night anyway, so I've told him that we're gonna have a ride back up to the roundabout and see if there are any rooms available at the hotel up there. It saves us cartin' all the bags 'round, 'cause if we don't have any joy we'll have to go into Ostend again."

"So what's up with that?"

"To be honest, I'm not in the mood now. I just feel like gettin' to bed. It's nearly ten o'clock."

We got back to the roundabout in a couple of minutes. I parked on the yellow lines outside and Lewis ran in the hotel to see if they had a couple of rooms available. After five minutes or so, he appeared through the glass doors of the hotel and came over to the truck. He jumped on the cab step on my side and grabbed the mirror arm.

"They've only got one room with twin beds."

"That's alright, we're not shy, are we? We've been kippin' together in this bloody thing for nearly a week. Get it booked."

"That's just it, he won't let me book it until he's seen your passport."

"Why not?"

"'Cause he's not allowed to rent a room to two men – he must think we're a pair of shirt lifters."

"Did you tell him that we're brothers?"

"Yeah, that's why he wants to see your passport," he replied.

I rummaged through my bag and found my passport. Lewis took it in, and in no time at all he was back out, holding his thumbs up.

Thank God for that!

I left Lewis to take the bags into the hotel while I parked the truck.

I parked alongside the marina and tried to jam the passenger side door as tight against the marina wall as I could. I walked around the truck to check that everything was okay and gave the guy in the dock office a wave. He acknowledged by waving back, so I assumed he must have been okay with where I was parked. I set off through the fog towards the hotel.

When I walked in the door, I saw Lewis talking to the guy on reception. I was quite surprised, I thought that there would have been a few more people about, with the hotel being so full. The guy behind the counter smiled at me as I approached the desk.

"He's happy now, as soon as he saw you come through the door he said, *'Oh yes, he is your brother.'* He's been worried."

We asked him if there was any chance of something to eat, or if we would have to walk back into Ostend. He said that the chef had gone home, but he would make us some ham and cheese sandwiches if we wanted.

It sounded like a good idea, so we ordered a couple of beers and sat down to enjoy them whilst he went to make the sandwiches. His name was Charles, and he was a really nice guy. He told us that he had retired, and was working the night shift on reception so that he and his wife could have a little more spending money, because his pension didn't really give them a comfortable living.

Not that much different than our pensioners, then.

He didn't look bad for a sixty-seven year old, and he made a pretty decent ham and cheese sarnie as well. He explained to us that, if the manager came in the next morning and saw two guys booked into the same room, he would need a good excuse or he would get the sack, because the hotel owner frowned on such things. Also, he told us not to get too excited about the ferry running in the morning, as it had been on the news that the dispute wasn't yet over.

After a few more Heinekens, we retired to bed and I immediately fell asleep.

Cheap Beer

The next morning, the restaurant was full and amazingly, Charles was still on duty. He told us he would be finishing at eight and that his boss was in.

"Everything okay?" I asked.

"Yes, fine," Charles said.

We said our goodbyes for a second time to Charles and went to sit at a table set for two. As we devoured the customary continental breakfast, I caught the eye of a rather smart looking guy walking past the restaurant door. He acknowledged me with a nod as he passed, and I couldn't help thinking that he must have been the manager. He was probably reassuring himself about Lewis and I.

Don't be daft, I'm sure he's got better things to concern himself with.

Back at the truck, Charles's words were ringing in my ears, because the dock gates were still closed, which meant the dispute mustn't be over. When I approached the dock office, a different guy came out and handed us an identical leaflet to the one we had received the night before, it just had different dates on it which extended the strike.

In the end, I had to concede that we would have to go

down to Calais and get the ferry, otherwise we might never get home. After the checks we jumped back into the truck and, with the usual crossed fingers and a prayer, she started up.

"Get your map out, Lew, and tell me where we need to be headin'."

Lewis dragged his map out from under the bed and directed me out of Ostend towards Calais. It was a beautiful morning, all the previous night's fog had totally disappeared. The sun was shining and it was quite warm.

We made our way merrily south through the little towns, one of which even Lewis and I knew had some significance to us Brits. Dunkerque. Or as we knew it, Dunkirk. We strained to see something, I don't know what we expected to see, perhaps an old tank, or a landing craft, but the war had been over for forty years or so.

After a couple of hours of pleasant motoring, we arrived on the outskirts of Calais. It was very built-up, with lots of huge, industrial units dotted about.

"Hey, have you seen that?" said Lewis, pointing through the windscreen.

"What?"

"There. Is that where they do *Eastenders*?"

Out of the windscreen, I could see a building with *'Eastenders'* emblazoned on the side of it in huge letters.

"Oh, I've heard of that place, they sell cheap ale to all the English that come over."

"Are we havin' it?"

"You're dead right, kid. We'll be able to make some money sellin' beer back home."

"Sellin' it? Who to?"

"Our Cliff, for a start. You know how he likes a drink."

"Oh aye. That bugger'll guzzle the lot! D'you remember when…"

And then he related the story that Pop had told us.

Cliff had come home late one night, at about three in the morning. He was banging around at the bottom of the stairs, so Pop had shouted down to stop messing about and get to bed. Cliff told him that he was trying to get a barrel of beer up the stairs, so Pop shouted to leave it downstairs and he'd sort it in the morning. But Cliff said he couldn't because he'd already drunk it.

We pulled into the car park at the Eastenders warehouse. They were well equipped, because there were parking spaces for trucks and coaches, as well as cars. We parked up and went into the warehouse.

It was full of all kinds of beer and wine, quite a lot of which were brands that we had heard of, and plenty more of which we hadn't. Some of the more popular British beers weren't that much cheaper than they were at home. Lewis and I decided that if our little money-making enterprise was going to be worthwhile, we would have to take the cheaper, blonde French beer and crates of Stella for the more discerning drinker.

We got a variation of wines to sell and drink, a big bottle of vodka for Maisie, and a whisky for Pop. Since Lewis didn't have a credit card it all went on mine, and we had spent about three hundred pounds altogether. I was hoping that we would be able to sell some back at home, otherwise I was going to be staying in a lot when we got back. We decided that the cigarettes were cheaper on the ferry, so we would buy them there.

We went back out to the truck to load our purchases. We had that much, it was necessary to load the beer onto the trailer rather than into the cab, where space was at a premium.

Back at the truck, it was surrounded by coaches that seemed to be full of pensioners who must've been over on a booze cruise. They were waving and pointing at us. I climbed in the trailer and Lewis started to pass the beer up to me.

The people on the coaches started to jeer at us as we

loaded the beer.

"Have you got a spare tree, love?"

"Have you got a big, bushy one for me, lads?"

"Cheeky old buggers," Lewis looked up at me, smiling as he passed me another case of Stella. "This is takin' too long and me arms are achin' as well. Hold on." He turned and walked away, back towards the warehouse.

"Where you goin'?" I shouted after him. He held his hand up behind him.

What's he up to?

He disappeared around the corner of the building.

I looked around, trying not to catch the gaze of the female pensioners waving at me out of the coach windows. Lewis came around the corner driving a forklift, and he pulled up alongside the truck.

"This'll make it easier, Bert."

"Where've you got that from?"

"'Round there," he said nonchalantly, pointing behind him.

"Did they say you could use it?"

"I doubt it. I didn't ask them."

"Bloody 'ell, quick. Get that ale lifted up to me and let's get it loaded before they come lookin' for it."

Lewis lifted the trolley up that had our shopping on it and I unloaded it in record time, then Lewis casually let the trolley back down to the ground and took the forklift back in the direction he had originally appeared from with it.

I jumped down off the truck and into the cab, praying she wouldn't let me down, as I anticipated the need for a quick getaway. I turned the key and-

Vroom!

Bloody brilliant.

I was scanning the mirror, expecting Lewis to come running around the corner being pursued by angry, French warehouse men, but he came sauntering toward the truck, and even stopped to talk to one of the old dears who had alighted from a coach. I gave him a quick *'toot'* on the air horns and he made his way to the truck and jumped in the cab.

"What's up with you?"

"What's up with me? I half expected you to be chased 'round that corner by a load of bloody Frenchmen."

"Nah," he said coolly. "They didn't even know I'd taken it."

"You're a rum bugger, you."

"Hey, how much d'you reckon we'll make on that beer and stuff?"

"We? WE? You'll make bugger all unless you stump up your share when we get home."

"I will, stop worryin', Maisie's savin' some money out my wages for me."

"What, about a quid a week?" I said, sarcastically.

"No, fiver a month actually, so naff off."

"Bloody 'ell! No need to worry there then."

Idiot.

We wormed our way through the streets and over the roundabouts until we finally arrived on the docks of Calais. It was quite impressive, in comparison to Ostend and Dover. There were a number of kiosks dedicated to trucks and each one had its own weighbridge, so it wasn't necessary to ride around to find one.

I pulled alongside the kiosk and switched the engine off, as instructed by the notice on the window. As soon as I did, a girl in the kiosk, who had a lovely smile said, "Bonjour."

Lewis wound the window down, "Alreet?" he said. I leaned across to give her our tickets and tried to explain why we were using this dock instead of Ostend, and that the guy at Ostend said we could use the ticket at Calais.

She stopped me and told me that there was no problem. She passed Lewis the necessary tickets, told us to park on lane thirty-five, and that we would be sailing on the *Pride of Dover* ferry, which was boarding in twenty minutes. As she was shutting the window, Lewis called over.

"Do we get a free meal on this ferry?"

"Yes, of course," she said, "with your meal vouchers." She pointed at the pile of tickets she had given to Lewis.

"And a bed?"

"A bed?" she looked confused.

"Y'know, a bunk in the cabins downstairs," Lewis explained.

"Oh," she realised what he was saying, "I do not think you need to sleep on this ferry, it only takes one hour and ten minutes to get to Dover."

"Oh, reet."

"Leave her alone." I turned the key in the ignition.

And my worst fears materialised.

The truck wouldn't start.

"What's up with it?" Lewis asked.

"I dunno. It's been doin' this a lot at home, but I can't find out what it is. It'll turn the engine over, but it won't start. It must be somethin' to do with the electronic stop control, 'cause it just won't allow any fuel through."

"So what do we do?"

"Sometimes, when you give it a minute and try it again, it just starts. But if it doesn't we'll have to tip up the cab and screw in a plunger on the fuel pump."

"Fuckin' heap. Fancy doing it here, with her lookin' at us."

"Aye, and you doin' your best to chat her up." I tried the key again.

No. She just kept turning the engine over and not firing.

We had a little queue behind us now, and the girl in the kiosk slid her window open and asked if there was a problem.

"Yeah, this bloody scrap yard," said Lewis, sinking into his seat.

"No, we're alright. It does this sometimes."

And then-

Vroom!

She fired.

"You old bastard!" I exclaimed at the truck. "Never a dull moment with you, is there?"

"Picked a right spot to break down, din't she?" Lewis laughed, nervously.

"Oh aye. Typical woman – likes a big entrance."

We joined the right lane and waited our call to start boarding. We hardly had time to have a smoke before we started moving forward into the huge, gaping hull of the *Pride of Dover*. We were one of the first trucks on again, so we ended up on the top deck. It looked like a fairly new boat in comparison to the one we had travelled to Ostend in, but since this was the main crossing route, it made sense to have the better ferries servicing it.

Lewis's Steak

On board the ship, I could really notice the difference. This one was much bigger, and there was a lot more to do on board, which I thought was odd, considering that you would spend less time aboard this ferry than the Ostend one. But as they say, it wasn't for us to reason why. The only reason I could think was, as it was the primary holiday route for drivers going to France or Spain, maybe it was to keep the kids quiet for an hour, because most of the entertainment was aimed at the younger end.

The truckers' restaurant was even plusher than the one on our outbound journey – it was much bigger and very well staffed. Lewis and I sat down and scanned though the menu. There was a considerable choice of dishes from various cuisines; French, Italian, Spanish. But even with such a cosmopolitan array of foods at his fingertips, Lewis was adamant that he was having steak – but very well done, this time – and pom frittes. I decided that I would have minestrone soup again, and carbonara.

"Carbonara?" exclaimed Lewis, "you know what Maisie'd say."

"*Bloody foreign muck!*'" we said in unison, laughing.

"Right, where's the waiter Bert?" asked Lewis, looking

around.

The waiter for our section of the restaurant was behind Lewis, taking the order of a rather large gentleman who was a dead ringer for Geoff Capes, British ex-shot putter and strongman.

"He's just takin' Geoff Capes order, so don't mither him or else Geoff'll fuckin' lump you," I chuckled.

"Fuck me, he does look like Geoff Capes," Lewis said rather loudly. "It's not him is it?" he asked, turning back to face me.

"Hey up, he's comin' now."

"Who? Geoff?"

"No, the waiter, you melon."

"Je peux prendre votre commande s'il vous plait?" said the waiter, arriving at our table.

"Sorry?" said Lewis.

"Ah! English. Can I take your order, please?"

After I had ordered, Lewis asked for his steak and chips, making it quite clear to the waiter that he wanted his steak well done – no, *very* well done.

"Well, how well done is well done?" he was asking the waiter. "I don't want blood comin' out of it, 'cause that'll make me heave." The waiter assured Lewis that he would convey his request to the chef. As he was leaving our table Lewis shouted, "Don't forget, very well done!" The waiter smiled and went into the kitchen.

"He'll probably cook your steak for about an hour now," I said, "it'll be like one of Maisie's burnt offerin's."

"I don't care, I can't stand it when all the blood is leakin' out."

While we waited for our dinner to arrive, we discussed our trip and all the helpful people we had met on the way. We remembered Lewis's gay, Irish mate Seamus, Bob the Geordie, the two Welsh lads, and many others without whose help we might have been in a wholly different position than the one in which we were in.

"Hey up," said Lewis, "He's here with our dinner." I

turned around to see our waiter making his way towards us, carrying a plate of food. "Here you are," Lewis said, pointing down at the space between his knife and fork on the table.

"That can't be yours, Lew," I whispered over to him, "it's only been about fifteen minutes."

"Pardon?" said the waiter, stopping at our table.

"Yep, that's my dinner," replied Lewis, pointing to the plate that the waiter was carrying.

I noticed Geoff looking expectantly over at the waiter, and he was glancing towards Geoff with a look of confusion on his face.

"Lew, I think that's Geoff's dinner, not yours," I said.

"Is it fuck Geoff's, it's mine. Put it down here, Pierre lad, and go and get me some vinegar for me chips," demanded Lewis, almost drooling.

"But Monsieur-" pleaded the waiter, as Lewis took the plate from him.

"Ooh! Just nice our Bert, I'm fuckin' starvin'," said Lewis, cutting into his steak.

As his knife slowly sank into the cut of meat, blood started to ooze out of the grain of the steak and run under his precious pom frittes. "Aww! Fuckin' 'ell!" exclaimed Lewis. "I said I wanted it well done, the bastards!"

"That's not your dinner, it's Geoff's. I tried tellin' you, but you wouldn't listen, would you?" As I was talking, I could see Geoff sat at the table behind us. He did not look a happy man.

"I can't eat this shit."

"Well, I'm afraid you're gonna have to, 'cause if you send that back Geoff'll fuckin' eat *you*!"

I couldn't help but laugh watching Lewis force tiny piece after tiny piece of steak into his mouth. He asked the waiter for bread, and every time he took some steak he would put a piece of bread in his mouth too, presumably so he wouldn't taste the steak. His beloved pom frittes were soaked in blood, and it looked like he couldn't bring himself to eat them. I told him it served him right for being too eager. I hoped that next time he might listen to me.

Poor old Geoff on the other hand, ended up with a piece of shoe leather that should have been Lewis's steak, and by time it arrived at his table he was in a hell of a mood. Hungry and angry, he kicked off with the waiter and got thrown out of the restaurant, which was a blessing for Lewis, as when this happened he felt he didn't need to eat any more of the steak.

"I feel sick," moaned Lewis, sounding like a child.

"Shuddup ya girl. My dinner was just nice. Are you havin' sweet?" I said sarcastically.

"No, I just wanna get out of here now."

"C'mon then, let's go and get some cigs from duty free and hope we don't bump into Geoff."

We left the restaurant and headed for the duty free shop with Lewis scanning ahead, just in case Geoff was waiting for him. We bought quite a few cigarettes, more than we were allowed that's for sure, but we stuck to the brands we knew – no more shitanes for us. A message came over the ship's tannoy system, requesting that all drivers to make their way back to the car decks.

"Bloody 'ell, got here quick din't we?"

"Aye, soon be home now our kid," I said.

Back on the car deck, we loaded Big Edith up with our shopping, hopped in ourselves, and turned the key.

Vroom!

British Customs

One of the deckhands started to remove the shackles. He must have been either French or Belgian, because he told me in pigeon English that our truck had made the whole of the ship's car decks smell lovely with the scent of Christmas trees.

We trundled off the loading ramp and followed all the other freight traffic. There were no transit lanes, all the trucks had to go through a tunnel which had yellow-jacketed customs guys standing about in it, picking trucks at random for inspection.

"Bloody 'ell, not again," I winced as one of the yellow-jacketed guys motioned me into a parking bay. I opened the window to greet him. "Alreet?"

"Hello guys," he said, nicely enough as he jumped on the cab step and looked in the window. "Have you got anything to declare?"

My mind flashed back to a conversation I had with Bob about duty-free. We were only allowed to bring back two hundred cigarettes each and a small amount of alcohol, definitely not the amount Lewis and I had on board. Bob recommended that if we brought extra back, not to try and hide them, just have them casually lying around the cab and be honest if we got pulled.

"Well, we've got a few extra cigs," I pointed at the ones on the dash and the bunk.

"Anything else?"

"Yeah, we've got some beer in the back."

"Right," he was quite stern now. "Where have you been to on mainland Europe?"

"Up to Denmark."

"Could I have your passports then, please?"

We handed our passports over and the guy jumped down off the step and disappeared into an office with them.

"Why didya tell him that we had that beer in the back?"

"It's just what Bob said, that if customs pull you, be honest."

"Well, I wouldn't have told him about the beer."

"You wouldn't have told him about anythin'," I felt an argument starting.

"How would he have known?"

"He could've climbed up and had a look," I added defensively. "Or, you never know, they might have cameras up there."

"Well, we'll never make any money out of that beer now, 'cause they'll want all the duty."

"You paid fuck all anyway, so I don't know what you're whingin' about." I was angrier with him now. He knew exactly how to wind me up.

The guy came back out of the office and handed our passports back.

"Cheers guys."

"Is that it?" I asked, shocked.

"Is that what?"

"Just get fuckin' goin'," Lewis whispered from the other side of the truck.

Don't fail me now.

Thankfully, the truck started and the guy went back out into the stream of traffic, probably to pull another truck in.

"What was all that about, then? He could've had us for extra cigs and beer." The only explanation I could come up with was that they probably had a database of people who go through regularly with more duty-free than they should, and since we weren't on it, they let us go. We emerged from the tunnel into a huge truck park, not unlike the one at Padborg in Denmark.

On arrival at Dover, I was under instructions to ring a telephone number for a shipping agent who we had to go through to get our goods accepted into the UK. I phoned the number and a guy told me where their office was on the docks, and to bring all documentation and the money for the VAT.

I eventually got to the offices of the shipping agent, which was a good twenty minute walk from where the truck was parked. I could really appreciate the size of the docks – they were massive.

I gave them all the necessary papers and the most important thing – the tax man's money. The two lads in there were very good, they probably had freight companies who gave them plenty of work and I thought we would just get pushed to the side to be dealt with as they saw fit, but I was in and out within fifteen minutes. They told me I had to go back to the truck park and take the T2 form and health certificate for the trees into the customs building, and they would get the VAT payment through as fast as they could. And with us paying cash, they didn't think the delay would be too long, but they said it could be an hour, or a day, because the customs and excise moved in mysterious ways.

You're not wrong there.

I was thinking of the episode under the tunnel earlier.

When I got back to the truck, Lewis had put the television that we had in the cab on. We hadn't used it yet because we knew it wouldn't work outside the UK. I didn't know what he was watching, but to be honest, I don't think he did either.

"Are you comin', or what?" I asked him when I opened the cab door.

"Where?"

"Up to customs."

"Aye, alright. Shall I bring some cigs?"

"Yeah, but don't bring them shitanes!"

"I don't think we've got any left, y'know."

British customs was very different from anything we had previously experienced. We joined a queue and shuffled our way along, very British-like, until we reached the window. When it was our turn, I handed my documents over with a smile. The miserable bugger behind the window looked at them, filled in a small piece of paper, and gave it to me. It had our truck and trailer numbers on it, and another one, which I assumed was our given customs number.

"Is that it? Are we cleared?"

"No," he said sternly. "You've gotta wait until you're notified."

"Notified? Who notifies us?"

"Can you see that screen behind you? Well, your truck number'll appear on there when you've cleared, then you come back to any of these windows with that piece of paper I've given you, and we'll issue you with a pass to leave the docks."

"How long will it be?"

"I've no idea. Your documents go to another office for processing."

We gave our thanks and wandered away from his window so he could see to somebody else.

"What's that place, Bert?" Lewis pointed to another room off the customs hall.

"I dunno. *'Sailor's Wheel.'*" I read the sign above the door as we approached. "Looks like a pub."

"Let's have a look then."

It *was* a pub, and the noise going on inside was unbelievable. It was a constant drone of truckers talking, probably swapping tales of individual journeys and all the different things that they had to endure to get their job done.

"I'll bet there are some interestin' stories bein' told by that lot, Lewis."

"Don't you mean some bollocks talked by that lot?"

It was a huge place, and it was full. It was funny, I could almost pick out the nationalities of the drivers. The Germans were all sitting together, as were the Dutch, Romanians, Turks, Greeks, French, and Italians. This was more of a European melting pot than the border at Denmark had been, the drivers here were literally from all over Europe. And looking around the place, a few of them were a bit worse for wear.

"I hope this lot doesn't hit the road at the same time as us," I said. "Hey up," a big moustached guy fell off his bar stool right in front of Lewis.

"Bloody 'ell, they're all arseholed!" The fallen man's colleagues staggered to his rescue.

"Are you sure you wanna drink in here? It's like bein' on a bloody pirate ship."

"Aye, why not? Could be a laugh."

It wasn't that much of a laugh. It was more worrying than anything, to think that every guy in the place – it wasn't open to the public, with it being a customs holding post – was in charge of a heavy goods vehicle. I had a coffee and Lewis had a beer.

After about half an hour, we decided to go back to the truck. We took a quick glance up at the screen on the way out, in anticipation of our number being shown, but it wasn't there yet, so we carried on back to the truck. Once there, we put the television on and decided to take it in turns to go back to the customs house every half an hour to see if we had been cleared.

A few hours passed that way, and by this time we had resigned ourselves to the fact that we wouldn't be getting home for a drink that night. It was five o'clock already and even if we did get cleared anytime soon, it was a seven hour drive home.

"No joy?" I asked Lewis as he returned from one of his trips.

"Nah, nothin'. I'll tell you what though, them drivers are gettin' worse. It's like Oldham on a Saturday night in that bar."

"Well, the sooner we can get out of here, the better."

"Pity we missed out on a drink tonight kid, 'cause I can't wait to tell the lads about this trip."

"Aye, it's been interestin', that's for sure."

"If we'd known what was gonna happen, we wouldn't have even set off, would we?" Lewis grimaced.

"No, you're right there, but it's not been bad, really. If there was any part of it you could change, what would it be?"

Without hesitation, Lewis replied, "This bloody truck!" and we both started laughing.

Homeward Bound

It was half past eight before our load had cleared customs and our number came up on the screen. Ironically, it was on one of my visits to check. I went to the window with my piece of paper, which by this time was looking like a mouse's nest, because of all the manhandling it had been through as we kept going back and forth to check the screen. I handed it over to the guy behind the window and he spread it out on the counter in front of him.

Just like Maisie does to a handkerchief before she irons it.

He pretended to struggle to make out the numbers, more to make a point of our untidiness I reckoned, and issued me with an eight-by-four inch piece of paper with our truck and trailer number on it. I was a bit disappointed actually, I didn't know why, but I was expecting a much grander document than this.

"Right kid," I said, climbing into the truck, "get that telly away and let's get goin'."

"Are we cleared?"

"Oh aye."

By the time we got sorted out in the cab and through the dock gates, it was nine o'clock. We decided that we'd drive as far north as Grantham and stop at the services, have a bit of a sleep, and get going at about seven in the morning. Hopefully, we would be back in the yard at Meadow Heights for about eleven o'clock.

Another reason we had for not going straight back to the yard now was that we wouldn't be able to unload our beer at four in the morning. And anyway, at eleven o'clock we could make a much grander entrance, which we thought we deserved.

Getting out of the docks was uneventful, we handed the slip to the policeman on the gate and he waved us through. It seemed strange to me now, driving on the left-hand side of the road. Almost as strange as it had felt over a week ago, on the other side of the water.

Funny really, it felt like I was missing it.

Eventually, we pulled onto the services at Grantham. We were both feeling tired and the sign, rightly so, declared it as a Welcome Break. I drove into a space between an English registered tanker and a Swiss registered truck.

"Well, nearly there, kid."

"Just nice," Lewis began to pull the curtains around the cab. "I can't wait. Shall we put the telly on?"

"Don't be daft."

Lewis got himself settled in his usual position between the seats and the gear stick.

Hey, I'll be in my own bed tonight," he mumbled sleepily.

"Oh aye," I agreed.

The cab fell into total silence. I didn't know whether it was because we were back in Mother England, or because we were genuinely more tired than we had been on the whole trip. We both nodded off to sleep.

Bang. Bang. Bang.
I jumped up with a start. "What the fuck's that?"
"Outside." Lewis was already sat up.

I pulled back the curtains to see a little old guy with a clipboard staring up at the cab window.

"Are you parkin' overnight?" he shouted.

I climbed down off the bunk onto the driver's seat and opened the window.

"What d'you want?"

"Are you parkin' overnight?"

"Well, what does it look like?" I replied flippantly, because I wasn't too impressed with the way we had just been disturbed from our slumber.

"Well," he glanced down at his clipboard. "You're not on my list."

"What fuckin' list?" I asked, getting slightly more irate.

"This," he said, holding his clipboard up to show me. "It tells me who's paid to park up for the night."

"Paid?" I said in disbelief.

"Yeah, it's twelve pounds to park one of them overnight," he informed me, pointing at our truck.

"Twelve quid to park up?" I blasted. "We've just been all the way up to Denmark, through Belgium, Holland, and Germany, and we haven't had to pay a parkin' fee once. Then we get back here and get fleeced right away."

"Well, I don't make the rules. I'm just doing me job."

"We're only gonna be here for about four hours."

"Dun't matter. It's twelve pounds for anythin' over two hours."

"Well, you can piss off." I wound the window back up.

"That's alright," he said, slightly muffled through the window. "I'll just take your truck number and they'll send the bill to your company for seventy-five pounds."

I had to concede. The old bastard had won.

"Don't we get a discount, 'cause we haven't been here all night?" I asked, winding the window back down.

"No, it's twelve pounds for anythin' over two hours," he repeated.

"Yeah, yeah. I heard you the first time," I said sarcastically.

"There y'are," he passed me a receipt for the twelve pounds I had reluctantly handed over to him.

"Do we get a free breakfast or 'owt with this?" I asked.

"You can have a coffee."

"Oh stop it, you're gettin' me all giddy. Do you have security on, then? 'Cause I'm worried about people nickin' trees off the back of the truck."

"No, we don't have security," he thought for a second and added, "the police come in for a cup of tea sometimes."

I wound the window up, shut the curtains and got back on the bunk. "Tosser!"

Welcome Home

We managed to get to sleep again and when the alarm went off at six thirty I felt more tired than I had done on the whole trip. We decided to go into the services and see what we could get with the voucher our friend, the parking assistant, had given us.

I could tell we were back on home soil – bloody miserable faces and crap food at an extortionate price. We got a free cup of tea and bacon sandwich each, but as usual they looked better than they tasted.

We ended up leaving most of the stale sandwich and stewed tea. We were walking to the exit of the cafeteria when I noticed a phone. I thought that I'd better ring the farm and let them know of our ETA.

Although it was seven thirty on a Sunday morning, I knew Mrs Mellor would be up and about.

"Hello, Meadow Heights, how may I help you?" came the familiar, croaky voice.

"Mornin' Mrs Mellor, it's Jack."

"Ooh! Jack!" she said excitedly. "How are you feeling? You must be tired."

"I'm alright, thanks."

"Have you eaten?"

"Yeah, we've eaten. I'm just ringin' to let you know that we'll be back at the farm around half eleven."

"Ooh good. Douglas'll be glad, he's been like an expectant mother ever since you left, he's been driving us all mad, you know!"

"Ok well, we'll see you about half eleven then," I was trying to get off the phone.

"Alright, I'll put the kettle on, will you want some breakfast?"

"No thanks, we should be ok, we'll have somethin' when we get home."

"Ooh! Your Mum's been worried about you, you know!"

"I know, I know," I said, wondering how to finish the conversation without being rude.

"Right bye." The phone disconnected.

Mrs Mellor wasn't being rude, that was just the way she ended phone calls. Somewhere out of the blue you'd get the famous, 'Right bye.'

Lewis and I had a walk around Big Edith to make sure everything was ok, and more importantly to check that our contraband beer was still there.

"All here!" shouted Lewis off the top of the trees.

"Good, let's get home, our kid."

"You're dead right, love," he said, climbing down off the back of the trailer.

Big Edith started up without any drama. I think she wanted to get home as much as Lewis and I. I steered Edith out onto the A1 heading north. The roads were quiet and strangely comforting. My thoughts turned to wondering if we might get out tonight for a few beers with our mates to tell them about our trip. Lewis must have been reading my mind.

"What d'you reckon Bert? One of Maisie's full un's when we get home, few hours' kip, and then out on the beer?"

"Sounds good to me kid."

"So, if we're back for about half eleven, home for twelve-" mused Lewis.

"Whoa," I stopped Lewis mid-sentence, "we won't be home for twelve, kid."

"Why?"

"Why? 'Cause you can bet your bollocks that Dougal Arse'll want these trees unloadin'"

"Well he can fuck off!" exclaimed Lewis.

"I'm tellin' you, as soon as we get in that yard, he'll want them off the truck."

"Well I'm tellin' you, he can fuck right off!"

"Well, let's see," I said, sensing Lewis's mood, but I knew Douglas only too well. "If we do unload them, it won't take as long as it did to load," I tried to placate him. "We'll just be throwin' the buggers off. C'mon kid, cheer up. We got this far, din't we? Should be proud of ourselves."

"Aye, I know," sighed Lewis, "it's just that *that* lazy bastard won't help. He'll just stand there, criticisin'."

"I know, here open them," I said, throwing a packet of Shitanes at him and smiling.

"Fuck me!" laughed Lewis, "I thought we'd smoked all these bloody things."

"No, I stashed a packet in the driver's door pocket for emergencies."

We quietly sucked on our Gitanes, occasionally looking across at each other with a grimace and a smile about our smoking material. We made good time back to Meadow Heights, pulling into the yard at eleven fifteen on the dot.

As I spun the truck around on the big, concrete yard, I nearly ran into Douglas when he came running out of the house like an excited child on Christmas morning. He was jumping up and down, waving his arms, and shouting at the top of his voice, "HURRAY! WOO-HOO! YIPPEE!"

He dodged the truck, forcing me to break suddenly.

"What they like then?" he asked, jumping up onto the cab step and forcing his head through the open window.

220

"They're ok, a good mix," I said, hesitantly.

"How much cash have you got left?"

Typical Dougal Arse. Money, money, money.

"Bloody 'ell! Have you had a fire in here? Bloody stinks!" said Douglas, screwing his nose up.

"No," I said, trying to stifle a laugh.

Good old Shitanes!

"Right, get it backed into the barn, and let's get them unloaded," he said, jumping down off the truck.

"Told you, didn't I?" I said to Lewis, straightening the truck up and reversing into the barn.

Lewis and I clambered down out of Big Edith, only to be summoned over to the farm house by Mrs Mellor.

"Come on, you two!" she beckoned. "I have made you a cup of tea and a sausage sandwich."

We started towards the house only to be stopped by Douglas.

"Where're you two goin'?"

"Your Mam's made us a brew and that," I replied.

"You haven't time for cups of tea, I want these trees unloadin'"

We turned to go back into the barn as Mrs Mellor blasted, "If you want to unload those trees, then you get on and do it! I have made tea and sandwiches for Jack and Lewis, and they are having them now. Another half an hour won't make any difference!"

One thing Dougal Arse didn't do was argue with his mother. He slunk back into the barn, head down, shoulders drooped, and started to undo the ropes securing the trees.

"Sit down and drink your tea," ordered Mrs Mellor, as Lewis and I entered the kitchen, "don't worry about him, he's like a child sometimes."

Don't I know it!

As we were tucking into our sausage sandwiches, Sally entered the kitchen.

"All back safe and sound then?"

"Yep," we both said, through sandwich-filled mouths.

"Have you had a nice time?" she asked, wafting past us to get the kettle off the AGA and fill it up with water.

Nice time? Nice bloody time?

"Oh yeah, we had a lovely time, din't we Lewis?" I said, sarcastically.

"You know what I mean," she said, smiling. "Anyway, more to the point, will *he* be happy with the trees?"

"'He's never happy with anythin'."

Just as I said that, Douglas came into the room creating an air of tension.

"Are you ready?" he asked, glaring at Lewis and I. "Paul's here. I've asked him to come in and help unload the trees, and I don't want to be payin' him to stand around, so hurry up." He turned to leave the kitchen.

Mrs Mellor rolled her eyes skyward as Lewis and I downed the last of our tea. We thanked her and left the kitchen.

"Get the forklift Lew, and bring it to the side of the truck and I'll load the beer onto it."

Lewis jumped onto the seat of the forklift and started it up. Douglas turned to him.

"What the fuck are you doin'?" he asked nastily. "You can't unload them with that!"

"I know," said Lewis, looking up toward me on the top of the trees, "we're just unloadin' our beer first."

"Beer? What fuckin' beer?"

"We got some duty-free for home," I said to Douglas.

"Duty-free beer? You've been fuckin' about buyin' duty free bee-" he paused for a minute, "you better not have bought it with my money!"

"'Ave we 'eck, it's our money!" I said angrily. "C'mon Lewis, get that truck over here."

Lewis positioned the truck at the side of the trailer and lifted the forks up so I could load our beer onto it.

"All this fuckin' about," mumbled Douglas, shaking his head.

I looked over to Paul, who smiled and made a 'wanker' gesture at Douglas's turned back.

Beer and wine unloaded, we began to throw the trees off. I threw the first one down butt-first. It made a thudding noise as it hit the concrete floor and softly flopped over. Lewis threw the next one down with the same *thud* and graceful flop.

"Hold that one up," demanded Douglas, standing there with his hand-held clicker, like some half-arsed gun slinger. Paul did as instructed whilst Lewis and I stood watching from the top of the load.

"Pull the branches down – fluff them out." He walked around the tree, studying it like a general would inspect one of his troop. "This in't a very good one, is it?" he said, looking up at me.

"What d'you mean? It's alright!" I said, defending the tree.

"They're supposed to be top quality, they look like rubbish to me!" sneered Douglas.

I was fuming.

You little prick.

You stand there lookin' at one tree in the comfort of your barn, when you have all the time in the world to scrutinise.

If you'd paid for top quality, you might've got it.

Instead of payin' fuck all, as usual.

"Just fuckin' throw them off," I directed Lewis.

"Hold on," said Douglas, "I want to look at that one too."

We stopped again.

"If you're gonna look at every fuckin' tree, we're gonna be here all bastard night!" I shouted angrily. "And if that's what you wanna do, I'm goin' home. C'mon, Lewis."

We started to climb down off the truck.

"No, hold on," said Douglas, "why you bein' so nasty? I only want to check the quality!" he added snidely.

Lewis and I clambered back onto the truck and carried on with the unloading. In between telling us exactly how many trees we had unloaded so far, Douglas occasionally selected a tree and dragged it out of the way to scrutinise it, shaking his head, and then returning it to the stack with the rest of the unloaded trees. To speed things up, we got some extra help from two young lads who worked weekends in the shop. They were hampered by Douglas telling them how to handle the trees, and to be careful not to break the tops or bang them down too hard in case the needles fell off. A proper aficionado of Christmas trees, was our Douglas.

The mood in the barn had gone slightly more congenial since Douglas had stopped whinging, so we were feeling better with ourselves and even having a bit of a laugh, whispering to ourselves and mimicking Douglas.

"That's a shit tree!"

And Lewis would reply, "Fully allowed!"

At that moment, Pop appeared at the side of the truck with Butch on his lead.

"Alreet Pop?" said Lewis.

"Aye, not so bad," he replied. "You lads alreet? Not got into any trouble have you? Are Interpol gonna be knockin' on our door?" he laughed.

"Are they 'eck!" laughed Lewis.

Douglas spotted Pop. "Hello Frank, how are you? Your dog's lookin' grey, why's that?" chuckled Douglas.

"Worry." Replied Pop. "What's your excuse?"

"Worry? Worry?" ranted Douglas. "I've got worry with these bastards, that's why I'm grey!"

Pop turned to us, smiling.

He knew how to wind people up, our Pop, and Douglas was easy pray for him. It was the last thing we needed right now but, true to form, as he turned to leave he said, "These are shit trees, aren't they?"

Douglas burst into a rant again.

"I've been tellin' them that they're shit! I'm gonna lose loads of money, but they don't care!" He carried on whinging and Pop looked at us and winked. We had to smile.

"I'll tell your Mam you're home, see you in a bit," he started walking away. "They were shit, weren't they Butch?" I could hear the smile in his voice.

Once we had finished unloading, Lewis swept all the fallen needles off the trailer deck and I loaded my beloved Ferrari with our duty-free. Douglas was in a much better mood. He'd finally conceded that we had a good mix of trees and that he might just possibly get his money back on them.

He was ecstatic when he realised that we had fourteen extra trees on the load. Whether Douglas had miscounted with the clicker, or we had loaded extra, we'd never find out, but Douglas was happy and that was all that mattered.

"Oh Shit!"

Customers had already started to wander into the barn and peruse the newly arrived trees. I felt kind of proud, knowing that a few days ago those trees were lying on the floor over a thousand miles away in Denmark. Now, courtesy of Lewis and I, they were in a barn in the UK ready to bring Christmas cheer to numerous families.

Douglas wasted no time and pounced on the unsuspecting customers.

"Mornin' love," he said, "these trees are the freshest you'll find, just off the truck, straight from Denmark! I picked each one myself, so I know the quality's top notch."

Bloody unbelievable.

He gave a slight look in my direction and carried on with his sales pitch. "Let me guess, you like a big bushy one, don't you love?" said Douglas, with a touch of innuendo.

"Right, we're off," I shouted to Douglas.

"Don't be late in the mornin'," said Douglas, carrying on with his Del-Boy style sales patter, not even looking over at us.

Lewis and I clambered into the Ferrari and drove

toward the gate. I looked in the rear view mirror to see more people going into the barn, where no doubt Douglas would be telling them about his hard work hand picking all the trees himself. I laughed to myself as I pictured Douglas surrounded by the Trolls. I imagined him whinging about the quality and the Trolls bearing down on him.

Now that would have been interesting.

"Tell you what our kid," I said, turning to Lewis as we pulled up outside house. "It's funny but I'd go again y'know, would you?"

Lewis looked at me smiling and said, "Fully allowed."

We grabbed our bags off the back seat, as the boot was full of alcohol, and we heard Butch barking, which meant that Pop must have been home.

Our return was a bit of an anti-climax. I don't know what I expected – the streets lined with bunting, all the neighbours out welcoming back Maisie's two conquering heroes? All we got was Butch announcing our return.

We went around to the side door of the house and pushed it open – it was never locked, even at night.

'Bugger all to pinch in here,' Pop would say.

"We're home," I shouted from the door.

"Oh! You're back then?" asked Mam, appearing from nowhere.

"No," said Lewis, "we're still in Denmark."

"Still a cheeky bugger though, aren't you?" she replied, smiling. "Do you want a brew?"

"Aye, and a full 'un each, please Mam," asked Lewis, gripping her around the waist and slightly picking her up.

"Get off me, you daft bugger. And shut that door, you're letting all the cold in."

"In a minute, we gotta unload our beer yet," I told her.

"Beer? I thought you went for Christmas trees?"

"Yeah we did, but we got some duty-free beer on the way back."

"Yeah, we're gonna sell it," added Lewis.

"WE?" I looked at Lewis. "You still owe me for your

half!"

"You'll get it, stop moaning," replied Lewis.

"Ee! I don't know," said Maisie, rolling her eyes and turning the cooker on.

"Hey! I got you a present as well, Mam," said Lewis.

"Ooh! What is it?"

"A leg of reindeer for Sunday dinner," laughed Lewis.

"It better bloody not be!" said Maisie, screwing her nose up.

"No, only joking Mam. It's summat nice," Lewis said, leaving through the side door. Maisie looked after him smiling.

She looked quite well. I expected her to look a little frail and tired after the ordeal with Vera's funeral, but she was a tough old bird, our Mam.

Lewis and I made several trips from the car to the utility room unloading our wine and beer.

"Hey!" said Lewis. "Hide them chocolates that I bought for Mam, I'm gonna surprise her later."

Lewis had bought some rather expensive Belgian chocolates on the Ferry, thinking that Mam could eat them whilst watching *Coronation Street*. He wasn't all bad, our Lew. He was a bit rough around the edges, but he had a heart of gold.

"Bloody hell!" exclaimed Maisie as she eyed the stack of alcohol. "What you gonna do with that lot?"

"Like we said, sell it. Well, some of it anyway."

"Well, if I was you," said Maisie turning back to the cooker and pushing sausages around the frying pan, "I'd hide it, 'cause if our Clifford sees it, he'll drink the bloody lot."

She was right. Cliff liked a drink and he wasn't too fussy about what he drank or who had paid for it. So thinking of damage limitation, we agreed that Cliff could have six cans of Stella and forty cigarettes. We went into the front room where Pop was sitting in his armchair checking the football scores, hoping he had won the pools again.

"Here y'are Pop," I said, handing over a bottle of D-Y-C Spanish malt whisky we had bought him. Pop eyed the bottle for a minute and looked up at us.

"Dick whisky?" he remarked, smiling. "You got me a bottle of whisky, called dick?" he laughed.

"It's not dick, it's D-Y-C."

"Yeah, Dick! Well, so long as it tastes alright," he laughed. "Did you get your Mam 'owt?"

"Yeah," replied Lewis. He raised his voice slightly so Mam could hear, "But it's a surprise for later."

Lewis and I sat at the dining table behind Pop's chair, picked up our cups of tea, eyed the stack of toast that Maisie had put on the dining table, and waited for our breakfast. In between cooking our long awaited full 'un, Mam had set about emptying our bags and putting dirty clothes into the washing machine.

"Nice brew this mam, haven't had a good brew for over a week," complimented Lewis.

"Looks like you haven't changed these bloody undies for over a week as well, they're disgustin'! I'm not washin' these buggers, they're goin' straight in the bin!" she bellowed from the kitchen. Lewis and I looked over at each other.

Can't be embarrassed by your Mam, can you?

"Whatever Mam," laughed Lewis, "is our full 'un ready?"

"Just wait a minute while I put a full load in." There was silence for a minute. "What are these?" Mam was still going through Lewis's bag. "Aw! Is it my present, Lewis?"

Lewis looked at me questioningly, as he knew we had hidden Mam's chocolates.

"Ooh!" cried Mam in disgust. "*'A Fistful of Fannies'*, *'The Italian (Blow) Job'*, what the bloody 'ell are these?" she boomed.

"Oh shit!" mouthed Lewis, as he realised what he had left in his bag.

Acknowledgements

Many people told me that to write a book is very hard.

Although they had never attempted to write one themselves, they assured me it was so. Well, I can tell you now. They were wrong. It is damn near impossible to write a book without good people to inspire you and bring out the best of your creative side for all to see.

Firstly, I wish to thank my wonderful and supportive wife, Jabeen, for pushing me when I lost faith and couldn't be bothered.

My little brother, who first planted the seed and told me to write a book – thanks, our kid.

Thank you to all of the guys I have worked with, had a drink with, and sometimes fallen out with, who gave me inspiration for some of the characters.

Jaqueline Abromeit (Good Cover Design) for being so patient with my constant changes whilst she designed the book cover.

Our glamorous models (you know who you are), thanks for putting a face to my characters and posing so many times, you divas!

Finally, a big thank you to Saarah Dost, my editor, who I love. She made me realise that I may be able to write a story, but I need a good editor to make it into a book.

Made in the USA
Columbia, SC
28 March 2018